Dream a Pony
Wake a Spirit

The Story of Buster
a Choctaw Pony Survivor

Sarah Dickson Silver

Illustrated by
Paul King

LUMINARE PRESS

WWW.LUMINAREPRESS.COM

Dream a Pony, Wake a Spirit
The Story of Buster, a Choctaw Pony Survivor
© 2015 Sarah Dickson Silver
Illustrations © Paul King

Printed in the United States of America

Cover Illustration: Paul King

Luminare Press
467 W 17th Ave
Eugene, OR 97401
www.luminarepress.com

LCCN: 2015950485
ISBN: 978-1-937303-57-0

For more information, visit www.dreamapony.com

Dedication

*This book is dedicated to
every child who has ever dreamed of a pony,
to all those who cherish and conserve
our nation's first horses,
and
to the memory of my father
Cecil Bunyan Dickson*

CONTENTS

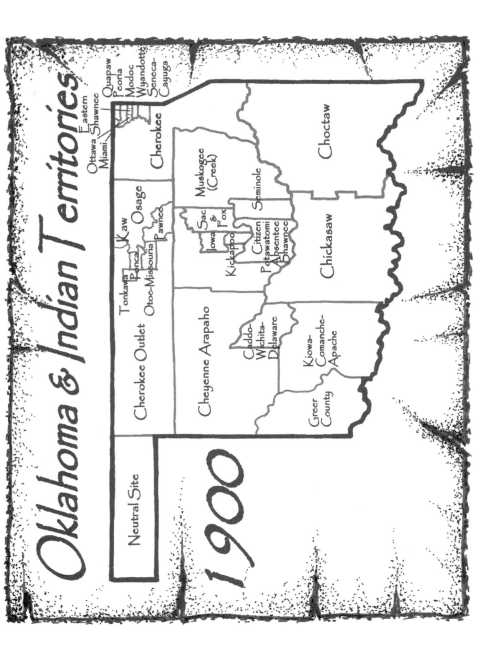

Oklahoma & Indian Territories

1900

Neutral Site

Cherokee Outlet

Cheyenne Arapaho

Greer County

Kiowa-Comanche-Apache

Caddo-Wichita-Delaware

Tonkawa
Ponca
Oto-Missouri

Kaw
Osage
Pawnee

Cherokee

Eastern Shawnee
Ottawa
Miami
Quapaw
Peoria
Modoc
Wyandotte
Seneca-Cayuga

Muskogee (Creek)

Sac & Fox
Iowa
Kickapoo
Citizen Pottawatomi
Absentee Shawnee

Seminole

Chickasaw

Choctaw

INTRODUCTION

*T*his historical novel was inspired by the stories my father told about his adventures growing up in Indian Territory, Choctaw Nation, at the dawn of the twentieth century. The star of most of my father's stories was his beloved Buster, a Choctaw pony he and his younger brother rescued from a death sentence. In these tales Buster was described so vividly that listeners could almost feel the pony's presence in the room.

As my father talked we learned what childhood in a dusty frontier settlement had been like. His storytelling brought to life the chatter and shuffle of the one-room schoolhouse full of barefoot children and their mixed cultures and languages. It made us envious of these frontier children's freedom to roam and explore at will. We wished we, too, could have played on the banks of their lovely Kiamichi River and have seen the wild horses roaming free there.

The period of the late nineteenth to early twentieth century brought immense cultural, political, and socio-economic change to the region that was Indian Territory and is now southeastern Oklahoma. These changes impacted the futures of all who lived in that place in those times. The pre-statehood history of Oklahoma, and of the people of the Indian Territory who fought so hard to preserve their promised lands and sovereignty, is well documented by scholars such as Angie Debo. Beyond the academic histories, however, are many personal stories of spirit, survival, and sacrifice that need to be told to every new generation. As the French historian Alexis deToqueville[1] warned, "When the past no longer illuminates the future, the spirit walks in darkness."

As I began my research for this book I discovered that there still exist a few hundred Choctaw, Chickasaw, and other horses of tribal family heritage. A core population of these horses is sheltered in the Antlers, Oklahoma area, not far from where my father grew up. These rare equines represent a uniquely pure strain of the Colonial Spanish horses brought to the Americas in the 1500s by the conquistadores, and their survival is gravely threatened.

In 2014 the Antlers area foundation herds, known as the Bryant Rickman Spanish Mustangs, were designated as the Heritage Horse of Oklahoma by the State Legislature. This has brought needed attention to their plight and strengthened efforts to sustain and protect their bloodlines from extinction. Videos and photos of the Heritage Horse Foundation Herds, and information about the volunteers, donors, and breeders who are trying to insure their survival, can be found at: www.thespiritofblackjackmountain.com. I hope you will access this lively website for more information.

Had I not met and received strong encouragement from Bryant and Darlene Rickman of Soper, Oklahoma, and from the prominent Choctaw historian Francine Locke Bray, and her husband, Michael, of Antlers, Oklahoma, this book would never have been completed. By sharing their infinite knowledge, generous hospitality, and deep commitment to these Heritage Horses of Oklahoma, they have made this

---

1   *In "Democracy in America" 1840*

book a communal effort. Collaboration with the noted Choctaw artist and educator, Paul King, has enhanced our effort. Thank you also to Gallo Crane Patel for his astute editing.

Others who have shared invaluable information for the book include D. Phillip Sponenberg, DVM/PhD, Professor of Genetics at Virginia-Maryland Regional College of Veterinary Medicine, who specializes in the genetics of domesticated animals, coat color genetics, and the conservation of rare breeds, and Ian Thompson, PhD/RPA, Director of the Choctaw Nation Historic Preservation Department, Tribal Historic Preservation Officer, and Tribal Archeologist.

Sales of this book benefit the Friends of the Heritage Horse Foundation Herds. This charitable non-profit is devoted to sustaining the health and well-being of the Heritage Horses of Oklahoma, as representatives of our country's first horses, and to raising public awareness of their centuries-long history, distinct equine characteristics, and deep cultural significance.

Sarah Dickson Silver

2015

PROLOGUE

Choctaw Nation, Indian Territory
Spring 1900

A CYCLONE COMES

◇◇

The half-grown colt had pressed close up against his mother. Feeling cold, wet, and very anxious after the two violent thunderstorms that had terrified him earlier in the night, he stuck his nose under the young mare's flank, seeking the comfort and sustenance of her milk. But the mare, who was already carrying her next foal, had weaned him a month before and now reached around with a sharp nip to reinforce that fact, even though she seemed happy to let him stay close to her. But his nosing around and bumping her bag had stimulated a little flow of milk and she felt that drawing down sensation as it reached her nipples. The colt, trying once more, was rewarded as the mare relaxed her leg and let him nurse, though she had only a little thin milk to give by now.

After the second storm had passed over them, the mare, the colt, the two big work mules, and old Ben, the man's bay saddle horse, had moved away from the barn. Now they were grouped together at the far end of the long narrow corral where the ground was slightly drier.

Annabelle, the sweet Jersey milk cow, was locked in her stall in the barn, protected under the heavy timbered loft.

The family's beloved flock of Barred Plymouth Rock chickens was roosting in the open side of the barn nearest the cabin, where there was no loft. With only a shingled roof above to protect them, the chickens would not be as lucky as the other farm animals that night.

The puddled path between the barn and the dogleg log cabin reflected the light from a waning moon, briefly uncovered by swiftly moving storm clouds. Moonlight sparked off droplets hanging on the wet wire fence that enclosed the little homestead's yard and garden. Early peas and greens were already well up in the garden, but a close look at the squash and cucumber mounds would reveal only a few brave tendrils, just poking out. Weeks ago the two oldest children of the Everett homestead had been assigned the task of building and then planting each mound with just three precious seeds, some of squash and some of cucumber, pushing them gently into the tops of the little hills. Every morning for a week now, they had run out to see if any of their seeds had sprouted.

But it was not the fate of these children to ever see their vegetable sprouts grow, nor would they ever taste the vinegary tartness of the cucumber pickles their mother would have made from them after the harvest. Nor would they get to enjoy eating the big yellow and green striped squash that would have grown from these mounds they had so carefully fashioned for them.

In the cabin, the same thunder storms that had frightened

the horses and mules had also sent the children scrambling from their pallets near the woodstove to climb up into their parents' high sided box bed that was bolted into the corner of the building. As they snuggled down for comfort, their father rewrapped the covers tightly around all five of them and then reached over the children and linked arms with his wife. Falling quickly and deeply asleep, they failed to hear the telltale roar of the approaching cyclone.

But Jethro, the lead mule, threw up his head when he first heard the rushing noise and turned to push the little herd even further into the far corner of the corral. Annabelle, the milk cow, was awakened when the chickens suddenly stirred and began to chitter nervously among themselves. Then she, too, heard the eerie sound and felt the hair stand up all along her bony brown back.

It came at that mystical moment just before dawn, when the birds first begin to chirrup softly and the air turns from solid black into a thick lavender infused with the promise of a new day. It came very fast, the long thin twisting neck of the funnel touching down just west of the garden fence. In the space of six heartbeats, it moved across the garden, scraping it bare, then plowed across the yard, leveling the outhouse, and glancing alongside the barn, lifting its roof right off. Then it paused for another two heartbeats directly over the cabin. The roof of the barn landed upside down just thirty feet away, but the cabin, and everything and everyone in it, was sucked up into the dark swirling funnel and disappeared.

THE HORSES AND MULES STAYED in the corral until the morning's warm sun began to dry their wet coats. Each one of them, Jim, Jethro, Old Ben, the pretty sorrel mare the family had called Flame, and her blaze-faced colt, had suffered some cuts and bruises from flying debris, but none was seriously injured. Now, at mid-morning, it was long past the time when the man usually came to let them out to graze. But the man had not come and they were hungry.

It was Jethro who spotted the place where the corral fence had been knocked down by a tree limb, and he led the little herd out over the downed fence and into the open meadow. As they grazed, the animals began to spread out. Old Ben hung around the barn area for a while hoping to see the man or the children and get the treat they usually had for him. But he soon gave up and wandered over to his favorite shade tree to take a very long nap, as old horses, like old men, are prone to do.

Jim and Jethro, being highly sociable animals, took advantage of their freedom to meander down the road about two miles to the Hinsdale's farm to visit with the mules that lived there. They knew them well because sometimes they would all be hitched together when one of the farmers needed to haul an extra heavy wagon load or plow up a new field.

The mare and colt stayed near Old Ben for a while, but then the mare, who was still feeling jittery and unsettled from the storm, felt an urge to move on away from the devastation of the homestead. She splashed across the creek and began to follow a deer trail back into the woods. The colt, suddenly realizing the mare was heading away from him, trotted to catch up to her. He was so anxious to keep close to her that when she paused at a turning on the trail, he bumped into her rump and she switched her tail at him as a warning to keep a little distance. The two kept moving on, the mare seeming determined to get somewhere else, and both were soon out of sight and sound of the little homestead. Old Ben eventually woke up and, finding he was all alone, nickered for the mare and colt, but they were too far away by then to hear him.

LATE THAT SAME DAY A neighbor of the Everett's came upon the sad scene at the homestead. Sam Goodman was on his way back from a two day wagon trip. He had picked up supplies from off one of the ferries that worked the Red River south of there. When he saw the barn roof lying upended between the road and the farmyard he brought his team up short in surprise. He had heard nothing about a cyclone during his trip. At first he could not figure out what had happened, but when Sam heard Annabelle bellowing in distress he turned his team into the lane to investigate.

Where's the house? he wondered. But the cabin was completely gone, and he could find no sign of the Everett family, nor even any wreckage. He did see a lot of dead chickens scattered around, and a few mostly de-feathered ones roosting pitifully up in the trees.

"How can this be?" he asked Annabelle as he milked her gently to ease her swollen bag. He only had one small bucket with him on his wagon, so after he had filled that he had to waste a lot of her milk just squirting it on the ground. *Maybe those chickens will find it,* Sam thought.

After he had tended to the little Jersey cow Sam looked around the place again without finding any clues to the mystery. He then tied Annabelle to the back of his wagon and climbed up on the wagon seat. He had just clucked to his team of horses to move them on when they threw up their heads and stared out to the left. That's when he saw Old Ben trotting toward them.

"Well, there's one more survivor," he said to his team and got down to greet the old gelding.

Ben seemed relieved when Sam put a rope around his neck and tied him next to Annabelle. Sam's farm was about three miles further down the road and he and his team were tired from their long journey and anxious to get home before dark. Nonetheless, Sam decided to stop at the Hinsdale farm to find out if they knew anything. There he found that John Hinsdale had turned Jim and Jethro in with their own mules when they found them visiting over the fence.

"I figured them mules had jimmied the gate again and Everett would be coming by anytime now to take them home," he told Sam.

When Sam described what he had seen at the Everett's the two men agreed to get up a band of neighbors to go searching for the family the very next morning.

"Couldn't have been blown too far, do you think?" asked Sam. "Dunno," John replied. "Kinda' hate to think what we might find out there."

By the time Sam Goodman finally saw the lamplight glowing from his own cabin windows that night, the mare and colt had reached a grassy meadow where they had settled in for the night.

EARLY THE NEXT DAY A few neighbors gathered at the Everett place to look for any evidence of where the cabin might have been blown to and of where the family might now be. But there was no trail of debris from the cabin, and no one found any evidence of the family members. Not even a shred of clothing or a pot or pan from the kitchen was discovered. Skunks and coyotes had found the dead chickens, though. Just a few smelly gnawed-on carcasses were left scattered around the yard. The few surviving hens that had been up in the trees the day before were nowhere to be seen.

One of the Hinsdale boys found the hoof prints of Flame and her colt where they had crossed Boggy Creek, but no one could take any more time from their own chores to hunt them down.

"They'll turn up in some ranch herd somewhere, or go wild," Sam said, and Hinsdale nodded in agreement.

While the other neighbors headed back to their homes, Sam and Hinsdale lingered, feeling they had to do something more. Finally they agreed between themselves to hold on to the Everett's other livestock, Old Ben, Annabelle, and the work mules, until they heard something about the family's fate.

"Don't see how they could be alive," Hinsdale said, "but their bodies got to be somewhere for somebody to trip over."

"Damn shame," said Sam.

IT TOOK CLYDE EVERETT ALMOST a month to get back to his home-stead. Sam's wife thought she was seeing a ghost when she spotted him walking up the lane to the Goodman's place. He carried a newspaper article torn from the *Arthur Texas Current*.

A MIRACLE: FAMILY RIDES CYCLONE AND LIVES!

TWO YOUNG MEN SLEEPING AT their fishing camp on the Texas side of the river below Arthur City had run for cover when a big windstorm came up suddenly. When they got back to the riverbank to pick up their gear they were astounded to find an intact corner wall of a cabin sitting half in the water with a family of five tucked in a bed next to the cabin wall, looking like they had just awoken from a nightmare. Clyde Everett, a white farmer, his Choctaw wife, and three children may be the only family to ever be sucked up in a cyclone and live to tell the tale. Everett is reported to have said he was giving up on trying to make it in Indian Territory and was going to move to Texas. "The Lord done set us down here so I guess he meant us to be here," he said.

Clyde told the Goodmans he was sharing the article with everyone he met.

AFTER SEARCHING FOR ANYTHING HE could salvage from the home site and barn, Clyde Everett traded Annabelle to Sam for an old wagon to which he hitched Jim and Jethro. He then loaded it up with what was left of his old life. He gave Old Ben to the Hinsdales for their younger children to learn to ride on. Clyde was headed for Grayson County, Texas where his brother had a store and where his wife and children had already been safely lodged.

"What about your mare and colt?" Sam had asked.

"If'n you find 'em, just keep 'em," Everett said. "I traded with some Choctaw kin of my wife's for that Flame mare 'cause Ben was getting mighty old and I figured I would need a new saddle horse soon. We didn't know she was in foal. Anyways," he continued, "I hardly got to ride her before the colt was born. But the children did love that colt. They woulda' spoiled him for sure, given time. I even found they were putting the youngest on his back and leading her around on him." He laughed and shook his head at the memory. "But I won't have any use for 'em where I'm goin', anyways. So good luck to you all and thank you again for your kindnesses."

And that was the last anyone around there ever heard from the Everett family. However, the story of their miraculous ride on a cyclone was told by those neighbors for many years and passed down to others by their children and their children's children.

FROM TIME TO TIME OVER the next few months Sam would ride down into the canyon to see if he could find tracks of the mare and colt. It was the colt he most wanted because of its unusual coloring. *Strawberry roan*, his grandma would have called it, with four high white socks, a big blaze and that silver grey mane and tail. *Fancy Pants*, he thought with a grin, *that's what I'd call him if he was mine.*

But Sam never found the roan pony and the story of what happened to the colt is one that neither Sam, nor any of the Everett children, would ever get to hear. Nor would they ever know that the life of that colt was later saved because he remembered being loved by the Everett children.

Oℵℰ

Luther Dreams a Pony

◇◇◇

*L*uther, his little brother Cecil and best friend, Joel, were watching three of their Choctaw friends ride away from their one-room schoolhouse on a big piebald gelding. "I wish we had a horse," said Luther, frowning.

"Yeah," responded Cecil, "and we could ride him to take the milk cows out."

For the past two years the brothers, now nine and eleven, had been herding five of the neighbors' milk cows out to pasture every morning and bringing them back every afternoon. At the end of the day, the cows, some with bags dripping milk, would begin ambling their way home single file and often met the boys halfway.

But recently the brothers had had to take the cows further from town in the mornings to find good open pasture. This rich bottomland section of Indian Territory was attracting more people, and gaining more livestock, every week. Twice this month the brothers had been late to school, even without stopping at home to dry their boots and pants cuffs after fording the creek.

"You goin' to ask The Judge for a cowpony to herd just five old milk cows?" Cecil laughed, brushing his mop of auburn hair away from his eyes to grin up at his brother. "

'The Judge' was the only name they ever called their father.

"Don't guess so," said Luther as he ducked his head down to hide the color that always crept up his neck and onto his cheeks when he was being teased. As he dug his right boot toe in the dust a hard little knot of determination was incubating; he could feel it in his stomach.

"But I'm going to get me a cowpony," he said, "you just wait and see. Somehow, I'm going to get me a pony."

Just then Joel's Pa showed up in their buggy to pick him up, as he often did. After they had waved goodbye Luther threw his head up, gave his little brother a playful shove, and started racing down the path toward the milk cow pasture. He stopped at the creek with his hands on his hips, breathing hard. When Cecil caught up to him Luther stooped down and let Cecil ride on his back. Luther teetered and swayed across the creek from one smooth rock to another, pretending to lose his balance. Then the brothers tumbled down in a heap on the far bank of the creek, laughing together, all teasing forgiven and forgotten.

When school let out that summer, all three boys began to take a lunch along with them in a galvanized pail and stay out with the cows all day at a little camp they had made in the cool of a cottonwood thicket. They would take turns bringing a book or a comic to read out loud while they lay on an old canvas sleeping roll, batting lazily at flies. They would drink a little warm milk tasting of wild onions which Luther had milked fresh from one of the sweet old cows, eat berries from the bushes that grew along the creek side, and listen for the trains.

In 1887 the Frisco Railroad had completed its North-South line from Monet, Missouri, to Paris, Texas, cutting right through this Choctaw Nation section of southeast Indian Territory. Decades earlier this Territory had been promised to Native American tribal peoples, many of whom had been forced to move there from their farms and plantations in the southeastern states. Nonetheless, a steady flow of non-Indians had also moved, legally or illegally, into this fertile section of the Indian Territory.

With the coming of the railroad, the area began to attract not just new farmers and cattle ranchers, but also people who could provide needed goods and services to the growing population, like storekeepers, bankers, preachers, doctors, and lawyers, and their families.

A few years earlier, Luther and Cecil's father had moved his family up from Paris, Texas to one of the new settlements across the Red River. Some non-Indian people were now allowed to live in the new town sites established next to the rail line. There, on what would become Main Street, The Judge had set up his law practice.

Joel's father had arrived about the same time to start the town's first newspaper. His printing press was used for posters and advertisements as well, including pamphlets designed to attract more businesses to the town.

The new settlement already had a train depot and there was a block of rough wood and tin buildings with false fronts and a section of raised boardwalk to provide relief from the mud and dust of the road.

On the north end of the town a few respectable frame houses with front porches were set back under shade trees. Scattered here and there throughout the settlement were log cabins of various sizes. Numerous shacks and tents accommodated the most recent or less prosperous settlers. Right alongside the rail line at the south end of the settlement was a series of corrals to hold livestock waiting to be shipped out to market. Close by the corrals were several large canvas and wood tent buildings that served as warehouses for the cotton, corn, and potatoes being grown in the rich Red River bottomlands.

Cecil and Luther had been the only Na Hullo (*white/European*) children in the settlement when they first started school, but now there were a couple of dozen, including Joel. Some of the new settlers wouldn't let their offspring go to the neighborhood school with the local Choctaw and Chickasaw children, but education was a priority for these boys' families. Having a good school was considered a privilege for them, just as it was for the Choctaw and Chickasaw families in the area.

Two

THE GUNSHOT

◇◇◇◇◇◇◇◇◇◇◇◇◇◇◇◇◇◇◇◇◇◇◇◇◇◇◇◇◇◇◇◇◇◇◇◇◇◇

*T*he Judge, although a good man at heart, believed in setting an example for the riffraff that he had to deal with from the Judge's bench. He felt it his duty to insure that his sons' behavior always mirrored his own strict standards, and he was quick with the belt if there were any deviations. Luther was protective of his little brother and was proud to take the blame, and the whipping, if they forgot to do chores on time, or were caught messing around somewhere like the rail yard.

Luther was proud of not ever crying, no matter how much The Judge's belt hurt. He also suspected The Judge did not hit as hard as he could have. He had seen the bloody welts on other boys' legs from the beatings their fathers had given them, and he had never gotten that kind of harsh treatment.

Joel's father, on the other hand, did not even spank him. He believed in sitting down and discussing things when problems arose. He called this method "finding common ground." Joel was also an unusually small boy with a very sharp mind who excelled in school and rarely misbehaved. He grinned when he was called "little teacher's pet" by his schoolmates, because he did not mind one bit being a favorite of their beautiful teacher, Miss Maisey. He did, however, mind being so small.

OUT AT THEIR LITTLE COW camp that summer, where no one could see or hear them, Luther would sometimes start to giggle, and then Cecil and Joel would catch it. All three would then roll around holding their stomachs and gasping as they recalled what had happened just a few weeks before. Even as old men, they would still be telling the story, prefacing it with the fact that "The Judge," was all of 5-foot-4 in his dress boots.

The Judge made up for his lack of stature by cultivating a larger-than-life personality. As a magistrate he was considered thoroughly knowledgeable in the law, but harsh and undeviating in his judgments. He was famous for scolding defendants as he pronounced sentence for such common crimes as claim jumping, rustling, thieving, lewdness, and public drunkenness. The occasional sentencing for armed robbery or murder brought crowds to hear him berate the guilty parties.

Earlier that summer, Stan Bailey, a not too successful gunslinger and rustler, had escaped from prison. The Judge had taunted Bailey in one of his more memorable pre-sentencing tirades and Bailey, in turn, had vowed revenge on The Judge.

Hearing a rumor that Bailey might be headed back to the area, The Judge began to carry a Remington army revolver with an eight-inch barrel in the right hand pocket of his suit pants whenever he left the house. Now, if you can picture how large that gun was relative to the size of The Judge, you will understand why he tended to keep his hand in that pocket, and on the gun, so it wouldn't bang his knee as he walked.

On the morning in question, The Judge stood up from the breakfast table at the usual time, removed his hat from the tall oak hat tree in the hall, and put the gun in the pants pocket of his best black suit, the one he wore when he had a trial scheduled. Since he had already given the two boys and Beth their orders for the day, he only nodded to them before opening the front door and disappearing down the steps.

Beth was one of the kindlier women in the series of housekeepers that had served the family after their mother had been sent to a hospital in the Colorado mountains to get well. Once the front door closed, the pretty young Choctaw woman allowed herself a small sigh of relief and a wink for the boys.

Cecil, the youngest, could melt her heart with his mischievous freckled grin and lively chatter, but Luther, the eldest, with his quiet calm ways and confident straightforward dark-eyed gaze, was her secret favorite. Now, with The Judge out of the house, Beth poured more coffee in her mug, and was reaching into the breadbasket for another biscuit when a gunshot rang out, very loud, very nearby.

"It's Bailey," yelled Cecil, "he's come to kill The Judge!" The boys jumped up, knocking their chairs about, but Beth was quick as a snake and had them both by their suspenders before they could get to the door.

"You ain't goin' out there," she said. "You get killed and

The Judge'll have my skin, for sure. Now shush. It's quiet. One way or other, it's all over."

"No, listen," whispered Luther, "I think somebody's comin'!"

"Comin' to get us?" cried Cecil, as footsteps sounded on the porch. All three were scrabbling for the kitchen when the front door opened and The Judge walked in, his pistol smoking in his hand.

"Did you get him, did you get Bailey?" the boys yelped as they danced around him. The Judge just stood there, looking past them, his mouth set thin and grim.

"Get me hot water and clean rags, and my bottle of whiskey," he ordered. "I've just shot the little toe off my right foot and I'm due in court in twenty minutes."

From that day on the old revolver was remanded to a locked drawer in The Judge's office desk. Much to Luther and Cecil's disappointment, the would-be gunslinger, Stan Bailey, never did show up...but the pony did.

THREE

FREEDOM

◇◇◇◇◇◇◇◇◇◇◇◇◇◇◇◇◇◇◇◇◇◇◇◇◇◇◇◇◇◇◇◇◇◇◇◇

On the days following the cyclone the mare that had been known as Flame had led her colt further and further away from the Everett homestead. At last she began to smell the fresh scent of other horses. Soon the pair was spotted by a wild stallion and his small herd of mares and foals. The stallion rushed at them with his ears back, snorting and blowing and circling and pushing them closer to the other horses. Within hours they were part of his herd, protected, but also dominated by him.

The other mares tolerated the two newcomers, but made sure they quickly learned that their places were at the very bottom of the pecking order. Then, later that summer, Flame gave birth to a pretty little filly that looked a lot like her, with a flame colored coat and blonde mane and tail.

Having a newborn foal seemed to get Flame more accepted by the other mares and she finally seemed content. The strawberry roan colt, however, was now a year old, and the old stallion, knowing that the young stud colts would someday challenge him, made sure these teenaged stud colts kept their distance from the mares.

But life was good out there in the rich grasslands and

the herd was healthy and strong. Whenever they spotted humans the stallion would quickly move the little herd in the opposite direction. But they sensed no real danger from the occasional lone rider on horseback, or from the lines of wagons that often rumbled slowly westward.

Eventually, however, the little herd was noticed by some cowboys from the big BRS ranch. These men then made plans to share the profit off this nice looking bunch of wild horses by catching and selling them. For a second time, the strawberry roan colt's life was about to be completely changed.

$\mathcal{F}ouR$

WILD HORSES

〈〉

*M*iss Maisey, the teacher at Cecil and Luther's one room school, had her back to the students while she wrote out an assignment on the blackboard. But like the conductor of an orchestra, she was attuned to every sound in every part of the room. Today, even with her back turned, she could recognize the whispering and restless shuffling in the older boys' section in the back left hand side of the room.

Yes, I have eyes in the back of my head, she smiled grimly to herself.

She carefully laid down the chalk on the rim of the black-board and silently picked up her ruler, her actions hidden from the students by the full puffed sleeves of her high-necked blouse. Turning around swiftly and cracking her ruler hard on her desk, she looked straight at the older boys section and caught them just as they were turning away from each other and trying to put on their "innocent" faces. The room became dead quiet.

All twenty-two students, from five-year-old Ida Mae to the big fifteen-year-old Collins twins, were now sitting up straight with their hands on their desks, feet together on the floor and looking right at their teacher. Most of them were eagerly anticipating that someone else was "gonna get it," and were glad it wasn't going to be them, at least this time.

"Older boys," said Miss Maisey, "please stand up."

Five boys, ages thirteen to fifteen, red faced and shuffling, rose to their feet. "Which of you would like to share your recent topic of conversation with the rest of us?" she asked, with considerable sarcasm.

There were surreptitious glances and nudges among the five. Finally Theo Collins, the more outgoing of the twins, stepped forward, nervously adjusting a loose suspender.

"It's about the horses," Theo stated.

"What about what horses?" urged Miss Maisey.

"The w-w-w-wuh-wild ones," he said, with a slight stutter.

A giggle and snort from the older girls' section was quickly silenced by Miss Maisey's fierce glare in their direction, but Theo had turned even redder and was looking at his feet.

"Thank you, Theo," Miss Maisey said, saving the boy any further embarrassment.

"Who would like to give us more details …?"

Wiry little Bert Spring, whose dad worked one of the large cotton farms outside town, stepped up.

"Thing of it is," he said, "my uncle Bud and his buddies from the BRS outfit, they done rounded up a bunch of wild horses and brought them into town. They got 'em down at the corrals and fixin' to start breaking 'em tomorrow. We was talkin' 'bout how it was goin' to be fun to watch and bettin' on who would get bucked off soonest."

"It'll be that big mouth, Curly," said Walter, the other Collins twin. But before anyone could challenge that statement, Miss Maisey said "Enough!" in her sternest voice.

"One at a time each of you go out and bring in a load of firewood for the stove. It's getting chilly in here. You first, Walter, the rest of you get back to your own work."

Turning back to the blackboard Miss Maisey failed to notice that Luther, instead of doing his schoolwork, was leaning back in his desk chair staring at the ceiling with a dreamy look on his face. Cecil noticed him, though, and guessed what Luther was thinking. *It's the pony,* Cecil said to himself, *Luther's dreamin' about the cowpony he wants, wonderin' if we can get one from that wild bunch. Oh boy, oh boy, he's gonna get us an adventure,* he thought, as he began to squirm with excitement.

"Cecil!!" said Miss Maisey, suddenly looming over him, "settle down or you'll spend the rest of the day in the corner." Cecil settled.

Joel, who had been sitting over in the littlest students section, teaching those children their ABC's, had heard and seen everything that went on, like he always did. He turned back to the children with a big grin and pointed to the letter P.

"P is for pony," he told them. "Sing it after me, now. P is for pony, puh, puh, pony."

Having a little person like Joel as a teacher made even the youngest and shyest child feel brave, so they were soon all singing along with him. Hearing this, Miss Maisey looked over at her star pupil and sighed. *I wonder,* she thought to herself, *what the future holds for this brilliant elf child. It's surely not going to be easy for him.*

FIVE

CAUGHT

◇◇◇◇◇◇◇◇◇◇◇◇◇◇◇◇◇◇◇◇◇◇◇◇◇◇◇◇◇◇◇◇◇◇◇◇◇◇

*B*ert's story was true. Down at the town corrals, there were sixteen exhausted and disoriented horses penned up. The mares with foals and the young fillies were in one pen. The lead stallion and the young stud colts, including Flame's roan colt, which was now nearly two years old, were crammed into a smaller pen at the other end of the line of corrals.

The cowboys had driven them steadily over a two-day period, allowing very few rests and very little water on the way. Each time the stallion had spotted a possible escape route the cowboys would be there with ropes swinging or shooting their guns into the air. Eventually, worn out and dispirited, the herd had been driven into the town corrals and separated. At least there were water tanks in the corrals and they had been thrown some hay. The cowboys had soon gone over to the gaming parlor to brag on their success, lay down bets on who would prove to be the best bronco buster, and sneak a drink or two in the backroom.

None of the other young stallions had ever been penned, but Flame's colt remembered the feel and smells of solid wooden post and rails from his early days living on the

Everett farm, and so he did not try to climb out like the old stallion and some of the other colts were trying to do.

EARLY THE NEXT MORNING SOME of the cowboys came back to take stock of what they had. A few of the mares, including Flame, had evidence of old saddle sores, patches of white hairs on their withers, or on their bellies where a saddle cinch had rubbed. Knowing that this meant these mares had been broken and ridden at some point, they moved them and their foals into another pen.

Then they put the stallion into the pen with those calmer mares so he would quiet down, because he had been constantly calling to his mares and raging around the pen, keeping all the other horses upset.

Two of the older cowboys sat on the fence smoking and discussing whether to try to break the stallion, or better yet, turn him back out with a few of the younger mares. That way the stallion would begin to gather a new herd from the many wild horses that were still out there wandering free. The stallion was a big boned horse with a handsome head and his offspring had proven to have a lot of stamina on the long drive, so the decision was easy.

"Well, Will," said Bud, who was the boss of the outfit, "let's pick a few of the mares and foals to turn out with him. How about starting with that pretty sorrel mare," he said, pointing to Flame. "She looks like she's carrying a foal and was broke, so she'll be our Judas horse. She'll make it easier for us to bring them in next time, 'cause she won't be as spooked. Then we'll give him that young grey filly from the wild bunch, too. She'll produce some good foals, got a lot of spunk and good feet and so does that big chested bay mare. You pick a few more good ones. That'll be a nice start on a new herd."

SOME OF THE YOUNGER COWBOYS now started straggling in, including the one called Curly. He had already been drinking steadily from a bottle of cheap whiskey that he had hidden in his oversized sheepskin vest. "OK, boys, pick your poison and let's get started," said Bud.

Will and Bud roped one of the wild mares and brought her into a larger corral, where she tried to get away by rearing and pulling. But the men kept pulling her closer using two ropes and she finally calmed down and seemed to listen to Will's quiet coaxing voice.

Meanwhile, the three younger hands, Curly, Jake, and Ben, had picked out a big three-year-old stud colt, who was already showing a bit of crest on his thick neck. It took all three of them to get him tied down and saddled, and the audience that had gathered to watch the action was jeering at them for being so clumsy.

In the next corral, Will had already gotten a makeshift hackamore on his mare and was working her in a circle on a long line, talking to her in a low steady voice all the time.

"Who's ridin'?" asked Ben.

"Me," said Curly, "I can ride anything."

The others laughed, but Curly jumped into the saddle and yelled, "Let him go!" He kicked the horse hard with his big Mexican style spurs, and at that, the horse arched his back, put his head down between his legs and bucked and twisted around the corral. Curly hung on for about four seconds and then landed hard on his rear end, just missing being kicked as the horse turned and continued to buck away.

The growing crowd around the corral laughed and whistled with delight.

"That no good piece of trash deserves to be kicked in the head," said Miz Palmer, who owned the gaming parlor. "He's a mean drunk. I had to throw him out of my place last night before he hurt somebody or got himself shot."

LIKE MOST MEN OF HIS kind though, Curly always blamed somebody else for the trouble he got into. This time he was blaming the young stallion, who was still twisting and bucking, trying to get rid of the saddle that was pinching his belly.

At that point the crowd's attention was drawn to the other corral, where Will had slipped neatly onto his mare's back while Bud held her head. But instead of bucking, as the crowd had hoped, the mare just sidled around a bit, her ears turned back to listen to Will's crooning voice.

Unnoticed, Curly had picked up a piece of broken fence rail and started toward his stallion with vengeance on his mind. The young horse was in a corner of the corral and he whirled around too late to avoid the first whack on his neck. Stunned, he dropped his head, giving Curly a chance to hit him again, this time across the nose. Suddenly, Curly himself was lifted up and thrown hard against the fence. Shaking his head and trying to stand up, he found Bud's big boot was on his chest, the piece of fence rail in Bud's meaty hand.

"You dumb fool!" shouted Bud. "This horse is worth money, or was. Now you've probably ruint him for good. Get your stuff and get out of here. I see you anywhere's near here again, I'll shoot you."

With that Curly slunk away and Bud yelled at his crew to tend to the horse Curly had hit and then get on with breaking the next horses. "Watch Will and learn something," he yelled at them.

"Heck with that," Ben muttered to Jake. "Will makes out like he uses Indian magic with them horses. I just think he's a coward, scared to ride a bronc."

"Well he's ridin' one now, ain't he?" said Jake, who was watching with interest as Will took his mare around the corral using just his legs and weight to turn her. "I'd make use of some of that magic, if he'll learn me."

Ben just snorted, but then he realized Bud, the boss man, was watching him and since he was working on the man's time he'd best do what the man said or he'd end up like Curly.

Sox

Curly's Fate

◇◇

Without access to Bud's string of cowponies, Curly was on foot, and no would-be cowboy wanted to be on foot in wild country like this. So Curly hid out in a nearby tent warehouse, drinking more of his whiskey, until the others had gone into town for lunch. Then, feeling brave and cocky once more, he snuck back to the corral to steal a horse.

Between his heavy drinking and his hurt pride, Curly's brain was not working well at all. Instead of picking one of the quieter mares that was probably already broke to ride, he went straight back to the site of his shame and roped a young strawberry roan stallion with flashy white socks and a silvery mane. He did have sense enough not to choose a big horse this time.

I'll pick something more like one of them little Indian ponies, he had thought. He figured he could bully it into shape right quick and make his escape.

When he roped the little horse he was surprised how easy it was to lead him out of the pen away from the rest of the young stallions. He jerked him around anyway, just to show the animal who was boss and tied him up tight on a fencepost. Again he was surprised the pony did not pull back on the rope, but just danced around a little.

"OK," mumbled Curly, "this is going to be easy." He went and stole the best saddle and bridle he could find from Bud's wagon and went back.

He had no trouble putting the bridle on the pony, except for the bit part, but still Curly figured it was his own skill as a horseman that was making everything go so smooth. Of course Curly did not know that this little horse had, once upon a time, been led and tied and brushed and his feet played with, and the littlest Everett child put on his back. Nor did he know that the pony had been much too young at that time to carry a saddle. So, when Curly threw the big heavy saddle at his back the pony shied away and swung around, causing Curly to stumble and drop it.

"Now you'll get it!" growled Curly.

He stood back, fishing the whiskey bottle out of his vest and took another long swig. Then he tied the pony's head even tighter to the fence post with Bud's best rope, almost cutting off the animal's breath. Finally, he took off his bandana and tied that over the pony's eyes.

"That'll fix you, you crow bait," he sneered.

In time, Curly succeeded in getting the saddle on the pony and started cinching it, but the liquor was making him careless and he did not tighten the cinch securely. He was near falling down drunk, but he fumbled himself onto the fence, let himself down into the saddle, and reached over with his pocket knife and cut the rope to free the pony's head.

The pony shook his head then, but did not move. He did not understand why he could not see and was waiting for the man to give him some indication of what he wanted. Curly swayed in the saddle, but caught himself by grabbing the saddle horn. Giving a cruel jerk to the reins he swung the pony's head around until it almost touched his knee. The sharp bit slid across the pony's tongue and cut his lip, and the pain dazed him for a minute. Then Curly dug his spurs into the pony's ribs.

The pony sidestepped and then backed up fast trying to figure out how to both balance the unsteady weight on his back with his head turned and escape the pain. But Curly kept kicking savagely, pouring out his anger at the way everyone had called him a no-count. Then, even beyond his rage, he felt a swelling in his head like a massive headache coming on. Suddenly, the pain was so severe that he dropped the reins and put both hands on his head and screamed.

With the release of the reins the pony began to move off at a quick trot and the saddle, which Curly had failed to cinch properly, slid to one side.

By now the pony was not only hurt, he was frightened by the shifting weight on his back and his blindness. When the saddle slid further, throwing Curly off to roll right under him, he instinctively reared up. Not being able to see where Curly was, the pony's left front hoof landed near Curly's shoulder and grazed his skull.

Still blinded, but instinctively trying to avoid stepping on whatever was beneath him, the pony reared again and the saddle swung around to hang under his belly, making him jump sideways once more.

IT WAS THE PIERCING SCREAM that had made people up in town look in the direction of the corrals. At that far distance they could just barely see a horse rear and plunge and rear and plunge again.

"Looks like he's stompin' a rattler," said one man, as he ran toward the pens.

By the time the first person had reached the corral, the little horse was free of both the saddle and the blindfold and was standing trembling on the far side of the corral, bleeding from the cuts in his mouth and the gouges on his flanks. They carried Curly to the nearest barn, but he had been dead before he ever hit the ground. The Doc, when he finally got there, said the head injury was nowhere near serious enough to have caused death.

"Hardly more'n a scrape," the Doc said. "That's not what killed him. Maybe the liquor did it, he was surely drunk enough."

But the Doc's opinion did not stop the gossip that spread all through the town about that sorry excuse for a cowboy called Curly who had been stomped to death by a wild strawberry roan stallion, a true enough man-killer of a horse.

$S \varepsilon \mathcal{D} \varepsilon \mathcal{N}$

FOUND

◇◇◇◇◇◇◇◇◇◇◇◇◇◇◇◇◇◇◇◇◇◇◇◇◇◇◇◇◇◇◇◇◇◇◇◇◇◇◇

Cecil and Luther had reluctantly obeyed The Judge when he told them not to go down to the corrals on the day they first heard about the wild horses. They were due to catch the train to Paris, Texas early the next morning to have Thanksgiving dinner and visit their Aunt Rooney, and they had to get to bed right after supper. So the news about the cowboy being killed by the wild stallion did not reach them right away.

Luther, Cecil, and The Judge did not get back home until very late the next night, so they still did not hear about the man-killer horse that day. The next morning, they got up extra early to take the milk cows out, and didn't see any of their friends then, either. So they still had not heard the news. But the boys were set on going down to the corrals to see the wild horses once their chores were done, and they were excited.

When the boys got back home from the milk cow pasture, they discovered that The Judge had already gone to his office and Beth was busy washing clothes out back, so they just took off for the corrals without telling anyone.

The town seemed eerily quiet and there was no one else

hanging around the corrals when they got there. Of course the boys did not know that most of the town folk, despite what they might have thought of Curly, were out at the cemetery, burying him. The funeral crowd was particularly large that day because, after the burial, they were going to be sharing a big spread of food. The new Presbyterian preacher and his small congregation were providing the food in hopes of attracting more people to attend their church services that coming Sunday.

Once at the corrals, the boys found the old stallion and the five mares that had been put in with him. They watched him herd the mares as far away as he could and then turn to face them with laid back ears and dare them to come any nearer. "Look at the old bite marks on him," said Luther. "I bet he's been in lots of fights with other stallions."

"And I bet he's won all of 'em, too," said Cecil. Moving on to the next pens they checked out the other mares and their fuzzy, shy foals, and finally, they found the younger stallions that were penned at the end of the line.

"Ohhh, look at that," Luther whispered in awe, "that one with the silvery mane."

"Wow," said Cecil. "He's just beautiful."

"Most beautiful thing I ever seen," said Luther. "But Hey! Is that blood?'

"Yeah," said Cecil. "Somebody must have rode him rough."

"Why'd he have to scar him up like that, though, that's stupid," said Luther. "And look, the side of his mouth's been torn, too."

Luther stuck his jaw out the way he always did when he made up his mind to do something.

"Well, this is our cowpony and they can't treat him that way," he declared.

"Wahdahya' mean he's ours?" asked Cecil.

"Cause he's the one I've been dreamin' on all this time, that's why," said Luther. "A strawberry roan, and look, he's got four white socks right up to his knees. That does it. Let's get us a rope. We gotta' get him out of there."

THE BOYS SCROUNGED AROUND IN a pile of ropes and saddles in the back of Bud's wagon until they found an old rope halter and tied a length of rope to it. When they came back they realized they could maybe maneuver the pony into the next pen—which happened to be empty—if one of them got behind him, cutting him off from the other horses, and the other opened the gate to the next pen at just the right moment. The next pen turned out to be not much more than a narrow chute, but it had a swinging gate that proved useful to hold the pony against the fence.

At first the pony responded fearfully to being held like this, showing the whites of his eyes and throwing his head up. But something about the boys, their size, their calm, quiet movements, and Luther's gentle hands, must have reminded the pony of the children he had known when he was just a young colt.

It still took an hour to first get the young horse to eat some hay from their hands, then to brush and comb the burrs out of his mane, and finally to find some old rags to wash and wipe away the blood that had dried on his flanks and his chin. By that time the pony's head had dropped, his eyes were calm and watchful, and he seemed to be enjoying the touching and the constant chatter of these two little boys. As they put the halter on, the boys were careful not to let it rub on his torn lip.

Then Luther said, "Suppose I get on him?"

"I don't know, you think he's really broke?" asked Cecil.

"Well, I guess it's the only way were gonna find out."

By that time Luther had already stretched his arms across the pony's back a few times, and leaned on him like he had seen a neighbor do with a young colt, and had taken one of the rags and moved it all around the pony's back and legs without getting more than a curious look from the pony. Luther had that feeling again, that familiar knot of determination in his stomach. *I am about to get me a cowpony,* he nodded to himself.

There was some nervous sidestepping after Luther slipped onto the pony's back, but Cecil held the halter and talked to the pony as he led him around with Luther on him. Then Cecil took a turn riding. But when they tried to get him to walk without being led, the pony seemed confused. Once he darted ahead when he felt a little squeeze on his ribs, and Cecil almost fell off. But soon the little horse seemed to get the hang of it and started walking out when they clucked to him.

That "cluck!" and a simple "whoa!" seemed to be sounds he knew the meaning of. Thankfully their shorter legs did not reach down to where Curly's spurs had slashed the pony's flanks, so they were not in danger of reminding him of that cruelty.

"There's only one thing left to do," Luther said.

"What's that?" asked Cecil.

"Show him to The Judge," responded Luther.

WHILE TALKING WITH THEIR FATHER on the train trip back from Paris, Luther had sensed that The Judge was at last considering getting them a horse. At least he hadn't discouraged them from talking about the wild herd that had been brought in. He even mentioned that he had heard that these mustangs made good cowponies and even buggy horses. So Luther had good reason to be optimistic as he led Cecil and the pony out of the corral and toward the street.

Cecil seemed relaxed on the pony so Luther let him move a little faster now and the pony broke into a stepping pace.

"Hey," said Cecil, "this is fun!"

"You know what?" said Luther as he ran alongside, "I think this horse is easy gaited!"

As the trio moved up the street toward The Judge's office they were proud to see how many people stopped and stared at them, and especially seemed to be contemplating the flashy little roan horse. The boys did not see the disbelief and concern on the people's faces as they passed, nor did they take notice of the murmured exchanges and the shaking of heads that followed their progress up the street. When they came to the gaming parlor they saw Miz Palmer out sweeping her porch and said "Howdy!" She looked up, stepped back with a little screech, threw her apron up over her face and ducked back indoors, shouting to someone.

"What's the matter with her?" Luther asked. Cecil just shrugged. They didn't realize that a number of people had started to follow them up the street. In fact, it was becoming a bit of a parade, including a few scruffy dogs, a woman pushing a baby carriage, and a couple of Miz Palmer's lady helpers with their fancy ruffled parasols and shiny bright colored dresses.

When they got close to The Judge's office the boys saw one of the men who had been lounging on the bench outside stand up, take in the sight of them, and then rush inside, letting the door slam behind him with a bang.

Just as they pulled up to the hitching rail in front of their father's office, The Judge himself opened the door and stepped out. He stood in the doorway with his thumbs in his vest pockets looking at the two boys and the little strawberry roan mustang for a good long time. Somebody was standing at The Judge's shoulder saying something to him in a worried tone of voice, but he brushed him away, and stepped out onto the boardwalk.

The Judge moved very quietly and deliberately down the steps to the street and let the pony look him over. Then he put his left hand on the pony's neck, stroked him, and trailed his hand across the pony's rump as he went around to the other side. He looked at the scars on the pony's flanks and ran his hand down one front leg as far as the fetlock. He raised his eyebrows in surprise when the pony lifted his foot for inspection. He stood at the pony's head and looked at its eyes and its ears, considered the torn lip, and finally rubbed him under his neck and down the chest to between his front legs. Then he stood back and looked sternly at his sons.

"Well," The Judge said, "you rode him here; you better take him on home."

If he hadn't turned to go back to his office so quickly the boys might have seen the slight crinkling around The Judge's eyes and the bare hint of a smile as he stepped onto the boardwalk and went back into his office, closing the door firmly behind him.

What the boys did notice, with considerable surprise, was the substantial number of people who had gathered around while the inspection was taking place.

"You'd think they'd never seen a horse before," laughed Cecil.

"Well, they haven't," Luther said with a big grin. "They none of them have ever in their whole born days seen a horse like this one."

"What are we gonna name him?" asked Cecil.

"Somethin' world famous," said Luther. "It'll come to us."

And they took the pony home.

EIGHT

THE EVIDENCE

◇◇◇◇◇◇◇◇◇◇◇◇◇◇◇◇◇◇◇◇◇◇◇◇◇◇◇◇◇◇◇◇◇◇◇◇◇◇◇

*T*hat evening, The Judge came home, took off his suit coat and hung it up on the wooden hat tree along with his hat. Then he sat down and pulled off his high-heeled boots with a barely audible moan and put on leather slippers. Next he removed the stiff collar from his shirt and laid it carefully on the front hall table. Then The Judge stood up, nodded to the boys, who were already sitting at the dining table, and went to the kitchen to wash up. The Judge came to the table, sat down, said grace, and looked up as Beth brought in the platter of meat and potatoes. Not a word was spoken while the four of them ate, but as he stood up to leave the table, The Judge told the boys to join him on the front porch after they helped Beth clear up.

Luther and Cecil exchanged a nervous glance because by that time they had heard at least ten different versions of what their killer horse had done to Curly, the cowboy. Each story had been more gruesome than the next. Even Beth was threatening to leave if that man-killing monster stayed in the backyard with Jericho, The Judge's old saddle horse, even one more day.

Now the boys' sympathy was all for the pony, of course,

since they knew he had been badly treated, but they did not know what The Judge would think about it. If the pony was really a man-killer, how could he allow them to keep him?

"They shoot that kind of horse, don't they?" Cecil had asked.

"And butcher them!" added Luther with a grimace.

The brothers waited in agony for The Judge to settle in his rocking chair with his glass of whiskey and his cigar, then they went out and sat on the edge of the porch. As usual, The Judge took his time.

"I'd guess you've heard the stories 'bout that pony by now?" he finally asked. They nodded.

"I don't think he done it," blurted Cecil.

"Did it," corrected The Judge, "did it, not 'done it'."

Luther rolled his eyes and gave a small sigh of frustration.

"Well," The Judge said, "you know it's my legal duty to find out the truth and I've spent the whole day hearing the evidence."

Luther wrapped his arms around his stomach, which was beginning to ache. He did not want to hear this. *I'll run away with him*, he thought, *I'll take him up the Kiamichi into the mountains and get adopted by the Indians up there. They won't care if my pony was supposed to have killed some mean white cowboy. They'd know just by looking at him it isn't true. It can't be true, it just can't.*

"Now here's the evidence," continued The Judge, "so pay attention."

Then, piece-by-piece, he recounted what he had heard and who he had heard it from. There were the numerous "eye witnesses" who swore they had seen the pony repeatedly stomping on Curly, but on close questioning those so-called witnesses had admitted they were too far away to see more than a horse rearing up a couple of times. Then there was the fact of the dead body in the corral with the horse. Now that couldn't be denied.

The Judge explained that there was indeed evidence of what the law would call "just cause" if the case were about a fight between two people. The wounds on the pony from the spurs and the sharp bit told their own story. "But the law doesn't protect animals that attack humans, even if they're provoked," he explained.

Finally, he told them about the evidence given by the doctor. "Now that is something we pay attention to because he's supposed to be an impartial expert. Doc says he is positive that the young man did not die from being stomped in the head. He's not sure what he died from, but the cut on his head was only a surface scrape and he didn't find any other signs of his being kicked or tromped on. Scalp wounds always bleed a lot so at first it looked worse than it was. Doc also said that Curly was heavily intoxicated, and the other men in Bud Talbert's crew agreed that Curly was near dead drunk." The Judge went on to say that Curly's heavy drinking, nasty temper, and bad character had been vividly described by Miz Palmer, and "some of her, uhm, young ladies" at the saloon.

"Then I have to add in the evidence you boys gave me," The Judge said

"What's that?" Luther asked.

"Why the fact that you rode him up to my office without

being killed, that's what. And then, of course, there is the evidence the pony himself gave."

"The pony gave you evidence? How'd he do that?" asked Cecil.

"Why he looked me straight in the eye and told me the whole story," said The Judge. "Didn't you hear him?"

Luther turned around and looked with astonishment at his father. The Judge was actually smiling! He could not remember The Judge smiling even once since their Mother had been sent to the consumption sanitarium in Colorado.

"You don't think he did it either!" he exclaimed.

"No," replied The Judge. "I think the evidence is pretty clear. The cowboy brought his fate on himself. It was no fault of the pony's."

"BUT that doesn't mean the pony won't remember," continued the Judge, "and that means you two have got to be very careful not to let him be reminded by anything you do or what anyone else does to him. He could still be dangerous if he gets that scared again."

The boys nodded. They were smart enough to know they weren't expert horsemen, yet.

"So," The Judge said, "Bud's sending one of his wranglers over to work with you some. He's Choctaw-Chickasaw and got quite a reputation for gentling rogue horses. I think Bud feels responsible for letting that Curly ever get to the pony and he wants to make amends."

"Amens?" asked Cecil in a puzzled voice.

A-MEN! thought Luther, who had just said a silent prayer of thanksgiving to the god of ponies and children.

MEETING WILL

◇◇◇◇◇◇◇◇◇◇◇◇◇◇◇◇◇◇◇◇◇◇◇◇◇◇◇◇◇◇◇◇◇◇◇◇◇◇

At breakfast the next morning Luther asked The Judge if they could take the pony with them to move the milk cows to pasture.

"No," The Judge said, "he's content with Jericho's company now and we have to make sure he'll be safe for you."

The Judge stood up and went into the hall to put on his coat and hat.

"You two just go straight out to the pasture after school and bring the milk cows home, and don't be dawdling out there," he said, frowning down at the boys. "I want you here when Bud's man comes."

LUTHER AND CECIL HAD TROUBLE concentrating on their lessons at school that day. They were overwhelmed with questions from their school friends —*When will we get to see him? What did he look like? Is he really a man-killing pony?* Miss Maisey had to settle everyone down to work with some harsh commands that morning, and she gave extra chores to the trouble makers during recess and lunch to keep them too busy to tease the brothers. When Luther came up to her desk and quietly asked if he and Cecil could be excused a few minutes early, she nodded her permission. The brothers were well down the road before any of their classmates could delay them.

LATER THAT EVENING, SITTING ON the porch of the house where she boarded, Miss Maisey heard several excited recaps of the incident of the two little boys and the man-killing horse. None of the stories seemed to be based on anything but rumor and speculation.

"All I can say," she told her fellow boarders, "is that the boys arrived at school unharmed, but far too distracted to pay attention to their lessons today."

"Well," huffed old Mrs. Bacon, their orange-haired, red-faced landlady. "I don't know what The Judge was thinking to let that murdering horse stay alive and be a danger to anyone he comes near to, and I intend to tell that to The Judge, straight to his face!"

Miss Maisey had to duck her head to hide a grin. Mrs. Bacon was always threatening to tell somebody something "to their face," but never seemed to find just the right moment to actually do it. Miss Maisey was thinking that she, on the other hand, was going to get to the bottom of this, one way or another, because her readers would be fascinated.

The fact was that, although she enjoyed teaching, Miss Maisey had a different goal for her future, one that she had not shared with anyone she had met here in Indian Territory. In her few private hours, she wrote stories for a newspaper back home in New England, and got paid a little cash for each one.

Miss Maisey wrote about her adventures as a teacher and single woman in this rough frontier town in the Territory, about the peccadilloes of the people she met and worked among, and especially about the children she taught. Miss Maisey had dreams of becoming a famous authoress, once she had enough stories. She was careful to write under a different name and never reveal the actual location where she was teaching, or ever use the children's actual names. She did not want anyone she knew here to find out that they had been the subject of one of her published stories.

As for Luther and Cecil, there was only one thing on their minds after they left school that day, and that was to get home as fast as possible and see their cowpony. Fortunately, the milk cows cooperated by being ready and willing to be herded to their respective backyard shelters, where the boys gave each one the portion of feed or hay she was supposed to have, and then raced home.

By the time they got to their house, Luther and Cecil were breathless from running and had to stop and rest at the front picket fence. That's when they realized they were hearing men's voices from the back of the house. The Judge's firm voice was easily identified, but they did not recognize the other quieter one. They tiptoed round the house and were surprised to see Beth sitting on the back porch shelling peas. It looked as if she had finished all the peas some time ago and was just going through the motions. Then they realized The Judge and another man were leaning over the paddock fence looking at the pony and talking.

Without even glancing back at them The Judge said "Come on over here, boys," confirming for them that their father had some extra-sensory power, because he always seemed to know exactly where they were.

"Meet Will," The Judge said, and the stranger gave a quick nod to each of them. The man was taller than The Judge and very slender and was dressed in denim work pants, work boots, and a long sleeved white shirt that contrasted sharply with his reddish brown skin and thick black hair.

"Will here is going to give this pony some training and I want you to watch and learn and follow his orders exactly. Do I make myself clear?" The Judge asked. The boys nodded.

"Speak up boys!" The Judge ordered.

"Yes, sir," gulped Luther.

"Um Hum," said Cecil, who was grinning ear to ear.

"Humph," was all The Judge said.

Then Beth noisily moved her chair and the Judge looked up to see her pointing to the big pitcher of mint tea she had set on the table. "Looks like we can offer you some refreshment," The Judge said to Will, and with that they all moved to the back porch.

LUTHER WAS A LITTLE PUZZLED because it was Tuesday, one of the days Beth always left early after putting their dinner in the oven to keep warm, but he and Cecil gladly drank the cool tea and ate the freshly baked cookies that had been kept safe from the flies under a bright colored cloth. The Judge then walked with Will out to the street and the boys saw them shake hands.

"I'm off," said Beth, hastily hanging her apron on the hook behind the door and grabbing the bag she always carried to work. "Your meal's in the oven as usual."

Cecil and Luther looked longingly at the four remaining cookies on the plate.

"How many you reckon The Judge'll want?" asked Cecil.

"Let's let him decide," said Luther. "Seems he's in the mood to make good decisions today!"

With that he took the cookies to the dining table where, later, after they had finished the main meal, The Judge gave the boys one cookie each.

Ten

WILL'S MISSION

◇◇◇◇◇◇◇◇◇◇◇◇◇◇◇◇◇◇◇◇◇◇◇◇◇◇◇◇◇◇◇◇◇◇◇◇

he Judge had made it clear that Will was to train the boys and the colt together, but Will wanted to be alone with the little horse for the first few times. He had some things to puzzle over and wanted plenty of time to do it without interruption. So on the first day of his mission he slipped quietly into the shed behind the Judge's house and got a wooden keg to sit on. He set the keg in the pen where Jericho and the colt were being kept, and laid a heavy bag down beside him. Then he sat down, tipped the keg back against the side of the barn and just watched the two horses for a while.

The main puzzlement Will was dealing with was the question of how this colt had come to be gentled, even though he had been found running with a wild herd. Will and Bud had spotted the wild herd almost a year ago and he knew this roan colt had been a youngster in the herd at the time. *But when and where would the colt, at such a young age, have had so much handling by humans that he allowed the boys to catch and ride him without fuss?*

None of the other young horses in the herd had shown any signs of having been handled before, but this colt must have been handled

53

by humans who were kind and gentle with him. They might even have been kids, come to think on it.

But where this colt had come from before he joined the wild herd was a mystery to Will and one that he knew would pester him forever.

Will studied the little horse closely. The shape of his small ears, the low set of his tail, the hard little hooves, the narrow, but deep chest, and the heavy mane and tail were typical of the horses he knew his Choctaw and Chickasaw ancestors had bred for centuries in their eastern homelands. So was the length and shape of the head and the size of the eyes, which shone with intelligence and inquisitiveness. The pony had a fourth gait, too; an easy to ride pace that Choctaw horses often displayed.

Will's people had bred these horses to be friendly to humans, even docile, so they would be safe around the children and kind to the elders. They had always kept their animals close to them, near their homes, and treated their horses much like working farm dogs; like part of the family.

In earlier times a Choctaw man's horse was often buried with him when he died so that he would have a horse to ride in the afterlife. Nowadays most people were happy to believe that the spirit of a man's beloved horse would travel with him into the afterlife, but that the horse could still be kept to help his family after he died. Nonetheless, Will knew some traditionalists who still practiced the old ways.

At any rate, Will knew his people's horses were bred for stamina and to carry weight far beyond what their small size would indicate. They also had to be able to do whatever job was required, from plowing to driving, riding to packing. Above all they were valued for their courage, speed, and their seeming willingness to serve the needs of their humans.

According to the stories handed down from generation to generation by Will's people, these horses had been part of their lives well before the English colonists had arrived in the country. The first horses the southeastern tribes such as the Choctaw, Chickasaw, and Cherokee had come into contact with were the small, compact, heavy-maned horses that had been brought to the continent in the early 1500s by Spanish explorers. It was offspring of those first Spanish horses that Will's people had begun their own herds with.

The Spanish soldiers had brought their horses to the Americas to help them conquer the New World. But Will's Choctaw and Chickasaw ancestors had always fought their wars on foot or settled arguments in the competitive stickball game they called "the little brother of war." They did not see any need for battle horses, so when they began to breed horses for themselves, it was for more peaceful purposes.

Will was certain, too, that this little horse and his dam, that flame colored mare, showed every physical character- istic of Choctaw breeding. That meant that this colt was not fathered by the stallion that was head of the wild herd they had brought in. That heavy, big boned stallion was not a Choctaw type of horse at all. Will figured that by some chance this colt and his dam had found their way to the wild herd from someplace else, someplace where they had known humans.

The second puzzlement that bothered Will was that he

did not know what really happened between this little horse and Curly. *I'll never know that*, he thought, *but I can figure out what kind of damage it may have done to this colt and whether that damage could ever cause the pony to be a danger to these boys, or to anyone else.*

Will got spittin' angry thinking about Curly. *Good riddance to him and his nasty kind*, he thought. *These pasty faced white drifters come out here to the Territory with their romantic ideas about the "wild west." They dress themselves up like Banty roosters in their fancy chaps and Mexican spurs, fuel themselves up on cheap whiskey, and think that makes them cowboys. What's worse is Bud goes and hires 'em 'cause he needs the extra hands and can't find anything better on short notice, but I am fed up with working with them.*

WILL WAS SO ENGROSSED IN thinking on Curly that he was startled to find Beth standing next to him with a glass jar of milk and a small basket covered with a plaid napkin.

"So you don't think the pony's a man-killer after all, do you?" she said. "Otherwise you wouldn't be here."

"Yep, I mean nope," Will said as he quickly brought the keg back to flat and stood up.

Will knew a little about Beth and her family. He knew that she worked hard and that her wages went to her Ma to help feed the younger kids, seeing as their Pa had taken off to parts unknown.

"Have some biscuits," she said with a warm smile. "I made extra this mornin' knowin' you were comin'."

"Yakoke," said Will, gratefully, and he watched as she

walked back to the house and raised her long skirt to go up the steps to the back porch. Then she turned and, seeing that he was watching her, gave him a little wave. With his mouth full of biscuit, the jar of milk in his left hand and another biscuit in his right hand, Will could only manage an awkward nod and a splutter of crumbs in her direction.

WILL BEGAN HIS MISSION A few days later by brushing the colt and putting some homemade ointment on his scars each day so they would heal over as smoothly as possible. Then he sacked him down and played with his feet and ears. Only when he was sure the colt had accepted him did he began the first lessons. He soon began to arrive at about lunchtime when Beth would have a sandwich and a cold drink for him and they'd sometimes share their stories and hopes for the future.

Will also had charge of training the boys on how to be expert horsemen. To fulfill that part of his mission he would work one afternoon a week after school and then sometimes for a longer time on Sunday afternoons. By watching first, and then trying it themselves, both boys learned to put the colt on a long line, taking him in circles, and then how to drive him by putting two lines on him and walking behind him. This was to teach the horse to turn at the lightest touch from the reins, and to flex his whole body when he turned.

"He'll need flexibility when you start cutting calves out of the herd with him," Will told them.

Will's next lesson for the boys was to teach them to ride bareback. Like most youngsters in these times, before automobiles were common, both boys had had experience on horseback. But they had usually ridden with a saddle. By riding bareback they learned to feel the horse's muscles and tendons working under them and to give signals with just a squeeze and by just a slight shifting of their weight. They were amazed to feel the pony respond --- like it was magic.

On those occasional Sunday afternoons Will would also talk about horses; how they see the world differently than humans, what effect being a herd animal has on their behavior, and what they do to protect themselves from danger. He warned them that they had to understand what horses' instincts are, "...because that's what they act on. You got to know how to use that knowledge to make the horse work with you and not fight you."

Will stressed that the worst thing you can ever do is to take out your anger on the horse.

"He'll never trust you if you hurt him. If he does something you don't want him to do, it will usually be 'cause you weren't watching close enough to anticipate it. You have to become one with the horse, meld your mind to his," he told the boys.

Eventually, Will began to ride out on Jericho, with one or the other of the boys on the pony, and expose them to rough terrain, to noise and confusion in crowded public places, and of course to the trains. Early on he had had the boys borrow some saucepans from Beth and march around the corral banging on them until both horses got plain bored with it and stopped paying any attention.

Whenever Beth hung out sheets to dry, Will made sure

to lead the pony back and forth in and around them 'til he stopped shying and showing the whites of his eyes. The bonus was that this exercise always brought Beth running out of the house to make sure that they didn't get horsehair on her clean wash.

One day Will even brought in a dead rattler and threw it on the ground. The pony snorted at it and backed away, but Jericho went charging right up to it and stomped it flat. Then the pony did some stomping, too, adding a little kick and squeal just to show off.

Finally, after about a month of training, Will informed The Judge he thought the pony and the boys were ready for each other. The very next morning Luther and Cecil rode double out behind the milk cows and then on to school.

"Well, look at that," said Miss Maisey as they rode up, "your infamous wild pony has finally graced us with his presence!"

Needless to say, the pony was a star attraction that day. Every one of Ida Mae's little school friends demanded a ride after she had been led around the school yard on him, and even Rilly and Josey, who were Cecil's age, had to take a turn.

The pony acted friendly and didn't mind the children's chattering and running around at all. Of course, no one knew that he had been raised around and loved by children, even though Will suspected it.

The little horse also made friends with the big old piebald gelding that David, Lucy, and Ida Mae rode to school each day and seemed content to be tied next to him at the hitching rail. He did throw his head up and take a step back when the school bell rang, because he had never heard that sound, but since the piebald didn't even twitch, the pony relaxed and watched the children streaming into the schoolhouse. He saw Miss Maisey step out of the door and look around for any latecomers and give a quick glance at the two horses. Then she shut the door and the noise from the schoolroom stopped immediately. That seemed to be the piebald's cue to go to sleep, so the little roan horse snoozed as well.

ELEVEN

A PONY BY ANY OTHER NAME

◇◇◇

"Haven't you named him yet?" asked Ida Mae a few weeks later, reaching up to pet the pony's soft pink nose.

"Still just 'Pony' for now," said Cecil. It was the noon recess and groups of children were spread around the schoolyard, some still eating their lunch, others playing stickball.

Luther was over with Joel, and some of the other older boys, reading comics and laughing. Joel's father owned the newspaper which meant Joel always got hold of the comic section days before it came out in the Sunday paper, and it made him even more popular.

Cecil was feeling left out, but too proud to show it, so he decided the pony needed to graze. He untied the pony and led him off to find a little grass. Lucy had done the same thing with their old gelding and Ida Mae, who had followed her sister as usual, began chattering away with Cecil and petting the pony.

Now Lucy joined the conversation.

"You have to name him," she said, nodding toward the pony "it's bad for him if you don't. It can be something that happened to him, or something he did, or sometimes just what he looks like."

"But Luther wants to give him a famous name and we just can't think of the right one," Cecil answered.

"Famous, huh? Well, killing a man is what he's famous for isn't it? Why haven't you named him Mankiller?" said Lucy with a wicked grin.

She knew the brothers had had to fight quite a few school-yard battles over the last few weeks defending their pony from that lie. Cecil turned red, but Lucy smiled and said "I'm just teasin', but give him a name because…."

Just then Miss Maisey rang the bell and recess was over.

"Because what?" Cecil asked Lucy as he tied the pony back to the hitching rail.

"Nothin," Lucy answered, "nothin' you'd understand," and she ran ahead.

Ida Mae tugged on his shirt and put her hand up to his ear.

"A spirit name," she whispered, "he has to have a secret spirit name, too." Then she ran after her sister.

Cecil stared after them. *What the heck does that mean?* he wondered.

In bed that night, after they had blown out the candle, Cecil told Luther what Ida Mae and Lucy had said. Luther got so quiet Cecil thought he had fallen asleep, but he was just letting that news sink in.

"You know, they're right. He is a spirit horse. How else did I picture him in my dreams? I knew exactly what he was going to look like… well, pretty close anyhow."

"So what's his name then?" demanded Cecil.

"I don't know yet," moaned Luther. He rolled over and was quiet again.

Cecil was startled awake a few minutes later.

"I've got it!" Luther was saying.

"Wha', what?" said Cecil, sitting up.

"You know today when Joel was showing us the new comics?" said Luther. "Well, there's this funny one about this long haired kid with a talking dog named Tige and how they always get into lots of trouble. The kid wears white socks and a fancy strawberry color outfit, just like our pony. He's already real famous in places like New York City."

"What's that got to do with naming the pony?" asked Cecil.

"That's the best part," Luther replied, "the cartoon boy's name is Buster Brown." Now it was Cecil's turn to be quiet.

"I don't get it," he finally said. "You think we should name the pony Buster Brown?"

"No, no, just 'Buster,' don't you see?" said Luther. "He busted a cowboy that was trying to bust him, he's the fanciest pants horse anyone ever saw, and he sure did get himself into lots of trouble... and you know what else? Will told me that Fritz, the butcher, had offered to buy him from Bud for the meat, and not just for the meat. He was gonna skin him and put the hide up on his shop wall 'cause it would be so pretty and sort of a trophy of a famous killer horse."

"NOOO!" cried Cecil in horror.

"Don't worry," Luther assured him, "Will wasn't gonna let that happen, even if he had to pay Bud for him out of his wages. Said he figured we saved him a few dollars by taking him off their hands!"

Cecil thought for a minute.

"Ok, so we name him Buster for the comic strip kid and everything, but what's his secret spirit name?" Luther leaned over and whispered in Cecil's ear.

"What do you think?" Luther asked.

"I think it's perfect!" said Cecil, and in minutes they were both sound asleep.

Twelve

BUSTER'S GUNFIGHT

When the shooting started Cecil and Luther were sitting up on the red leather swivel stools at Gibbs drugstore on Main Street sharing a vanilla shake. Suddenly there was a sudden rush of people coming into the store through the big glass front doors. Some women were shrieking and someone was yelling "Get Back! Stay Down!"

"What's happening?" shouted Mr. Gibbs from behind the counter.

"It's Chet Rogers and that young Brady boy fightin' again," said old Abe Smith, who had just made it through the door. "And this time they're gonna' kill each other for sure."

Luther and Cecil looked wide-eyed at each other, both thinking the same thing. They jumped down and ran toward the doors.

"Hey, get back here," said Abe as he grabbed both boys. "You cain't go out there, it's a gunfight!"

"But it's Buster," Cecil yelled. "He's tied out there, right across the street."

Then another shot rang out and Mr. Gibbs was suddenly there slamming the doors shut and turning around to block their escape.

"Now everybody just stay inside and hush up," he ordered. "If those two troublemakers want to kill each other it's fine with me. I'd call it thinning the herd, myself."

This got a laugh from the crowd and everyone moved upfront to watch the action. Luther and Cecil slipped around unnoticed and climbed into the display window to get a better view to the street.

Buster and a couple of other horses were tied at hitching rails on the other side of the street. Buster was a block away from the other two, placed right in front of The Judge's law office, as usual. The boys could see the pony was pulling back on the tie rope, trying to get loose. *C'mon Buster,* Luther thought, *you done it enough times before!*

But with a sinking heart Luther realized the pony was not going to get free this time. It had taken the boys many tries to perfect a knot that Buster couldn't figure out how to untie. When they had gotten into town that day they had been sure to get the knot tied just right so they would have a ride back.

Buster had left them stranded before, forcing them to make the long hot walk home. Once there, they'd find Buster standing happily at the corral gate, passing the time of day with Jericho, and just waiting patiently to be let in. Then he'd turn his head and look at them as if to say *"What took you two so long??'*

Suddenly the boys spotted Rogers slipping from behind the mercantile store on the corner and starting to inch up the boardwalk, a big six-shooter in his right hand.

"Oh," gasped Cecil, "and there's Brady up by the feed store, hiding behind that barrel!"

Suddenly Brady moved out to the street and fired. Rogers took the shot in his right leg, fell on the boardwalk and rolled off onto the dusty street right beside where Buster was tied. Then Rogers reached up and grabbed one of the pony's stirrups with his left hand to steady himself and with his gun held right under the pony's belly fired three shots in a row at Brady.

Brady went down looking like he had been hit, and Rogers started to crawl away to avoid the pony's hooves. Buster was bouncing around kicking up a storm of dust. Suddenly there were people dragging both men out of the street and the excitement was over.

"Did you see that?" whispered Luther.

Just then the door to their father's office opened, and The Judge stepped out all calm and cool as usual. First he stared hard at Buster, and then he slowly looked up the street to the left, then down the street to the right.

"He's checking to see if we're lying dead out there," laughed Luther.

Then, seemingly satisfied, The Judge turned and went back into the building, shutting the door firmly behind him. The boys tore out of the drugstore then, but when they reached Buster he was still prancing around and tossing his head and showing the whites of his eyes. Luther stood there with his tongue stuck into the left corner of his mouth like he always did when he was thinking hard.

"Tell you what, Cecil," he said thoughtfully, "Maybe we oughta' take turns leadin' and ridin' on the way home."

"Yeah," agreed Cecil, "I'm 'rememberin' what Will told

us, 'If you wanna' avoid a wreck, you got to always consider what's goin' on in your pony's head at that very moment' and if it's anythin' like what's goin' on in my head right now, I'd just as soon we lead him all the way home!"

And so they did.

THE BOYS HAD NOT NOTICED that Will was one of the people who had pulled the two gunfighters off the street and was now kneeling by Brady, who, it turned out, was one of the young cowboys from his ranch outfit. Will had been glad to see that Brady wasn't seriously wounded, but he had seen how Rogers had used Buster as a shield.

Will stood up and watched the boys leading the pony away and gave them a little nod of approval.

"I just might make decent horsemen outa' them boys after all," he murmured. "S'long as they keep usin' their heads like this."

JOEL WAS WATCHING HIS FRIENDS leave, too. He had seen the action from the vantage point of the second floor loading doors of the feed store. That was his favorite place to hang out because from that high up he could see all the comings and goings of the town. Now all Joel's thoughts were about how happy Miss Maisey would be to read his next school report, which of course would be about the gunfight. He ran quickly down the stairs and positioned himself in a dark corner near the benches around the stove, where he knew people would soon be gathering around and gossiping about

Brady and Rogers and what the fight was all about.

Miss Maisey had taught him to include all the background information, not just the action part of the story, and he could hardly wait to start writing. Whenever Miss Maisey read one of his reports she would point out the parts that were written best and suggest parts where changes were needed, just like his Pa did with his newspaper reporters. Then Miss Maisey would give him a smile so powerful it made him feel six feet tall.

THIRTEEN

BUSTER TO THE RESCUE

One morning a few weeks later, just as Luther and Cecil rode into the schoolyard, they saw Miss Maisey leaning over someone who was lying on the porch. It was Lucy. Ida Mae was sobbing and their old gelding was off in the grass with the reins dragging. Obviously something terrible had happened.

Miss Maisey looked up as they slid off Buster and came near to see what was happening.

"Lucy has a broken arm," she said, trying to keep her voice calm and steady. "Luther, I'm going to need you to ride out to the Thurman's place and tell them to come with a wagon. Better take the old gelding with you, they might need him."

Joel had already gone to catch the old horse. Although he and Luther were the same age, Joel was not much bigger than Ida Mae, but he was fearless around horses. Luther asked him what happened, and why Lucy and Ida Mae's big brother, David, wasn't there.

"David was needed on the farm today, so Lucy and Ida rode here alone," Joel told him. "Ida Mae said the horse shied at something and tossed them off just up the road. I think

Lucy was thrown against a tree or something. Miss Maisey already sent Theo and Walter to get the Doc."

Miss Maisey called Luther over.

"Can you do this alone?" she asked. "I really need Cecil and Joel to stay and help me with the younger children."

"Yes, Buster and me can do it," said Luther, with more confidence than he felt.

"Now try to reassure Lucy's parents. It's only a broken bone. The doctor will be on his way. It's just…" Miss Maisey pressed her lips tightly together to keep from crying, "It's just that she's in a lot of pain. She's a very brave girl, but she needs her mama. Get going now."

LUTHER GOT BACK ON BUSTER, and Joel handed the old piebald horse's reins to him. He clucked twice to Buster and they took off up the road at a lope. Buster hadn't even broken a sweat when the old piebald began to slow down, his breath sounding wheezy. Luther realized this wasn't going to be the exciting non-stop Pony Express ride he had imagined. The ancient old horse needed to take it much slower. *I don't know why Miss Maisey thought I should bring him,* he thought. *I could make it twice as fast without him.*

Suddenly the gelding's reins were ripped out of Luther's hand. The old gelding had stopped dead and was backing up, his nostrils wide and his eyes focused on a spot at the side of the road, just in front of Buster. Before Luther realized that a rattlesnake was coiled there, Buster reared up and slammed down on the snake with his front hooves. Luther was trying to get his feet back in his stirrups when Buster reared again, this time reducing the snake to mush. Only a frantic grab of mane and saddle horn had saved Luther from a fall. Buster snorted and danced around as if to say *Come on, snake, try it again.*

"Whoa!" shouted Luther, "Stop already, he's dead, you already killed it dead! And how about giving me some warning next time, you nutcase!"

Luther's heart was beating hard and he had to take a couple of deep breaths to clear his head. Then he realized the old gelding had disappeared. He continued on, worried now, but the piebald was just around the corner happily munching grass as if nothing whatever had happened.

"Got Buster to do your fighting for you, didn't you, you old coward," Luther said with a big grin and a pat on the neck for his brave pony.

As the trio started on down the road again, Luther had a disturbing thought. Buster had killed that snake the same way he was supposed to have killed Curly. *I know the Doc says Buster didn't kill him,* he thought, *but could he have meant to kill him and just missed?*

Luther tried to force that unpleasant image out of his head as they moved on down the road, but he felt like a little piece of his heart had been bruised. Would he never be able to really trust his pony? He knew he had dreamed about Buster and what he was going to look like, but what about his heart and spirit? Was this pony kind and courageous like he and Cecil thought, or was he angry and dangerous somewhere deep inside?

"I guess you'll show me, sooner or later," he said out

loud. Buster tipped an ear back to hear him and gave a snort.

At the slow pace the old horse now forced them to keep, it took a long time for them to come within sight of Lucy's home place. Luther saw several men working out in the fields and smoke coming from the stone chimney of the big cabin. As he turned into their long dusty lane Luther urged Buster into his pacing gait and the old gelding started an eager trot with his ears perked forward.

"Glad to be home, aren't you, old boy?" Luther said to the piebald.

Two of the men from the field were now running toward the house and a woman had come out of the doorway of the cabin into the yard. Luther had never met Lucy's mother, but he knew the taller man was her father because he sometimes drove the children to school in his wagon if he was heading for town that day. As they got closer the other man turned out to be David, Lucy's older brother. David darted ahead of his father and met Luther before he got as far as the house and took hold of the gelding, but he didn't ask anything, just ran alongside until they reached his parents.

When Luther told them the news about Lucy's broken arm, Lucy's father just nodded and, although Lucy's mother wrapped her hands nervously in her apron, she did not ask any questions. David said, "I'll see to the mules" and he and his father headed toward the barn.

Lucy's mother disappeared into the house, leaving Luther standing there, not knowing what to do next. He tied Buster to a hitching rail at the side of the large cabin and loosened his girth. Suddenly a young woman appeared on the porch, gesturing him to come. She offered him a tin cup and pointed to a crock full of water. The water was cool, as if fresh from a spring, and it tasted of lemon balm.

"Yakoke, thank you for coming," she said. "Glad to," Luther mumbled as he dipped his cup again. "I'll need to water my horse before I go back."

"Amafo, my grandfather, is seeing to him," the young woman answered. Luther turned to see Buster being led off by a very old man, all bent and crippled and leaning on a walking stick.

"I can do it," Luther said, concerned at how frail the old man looked. The young woman put a hand on his arm.

"Let him," she said, "it is his way of thanking you and he wants to tell you something."

So Luther stayed with the young woman until the old man had hobbled back, Buster trailing him as if he had known him forever. Leaning on his stick with two hands the old man peered up at Luther and began speaking in Choctaw. Luther had picked up some of the language from hearing his schoolmates talk, but the only words he understood now were *Chata* and *issuba,* the words for Choctaw and horse, and maybe there was something about a dog and a spirit. The old man stopped talking and looked expectantly at Luther. The young woman spoke softly behind him. "Grandfather says your horse is from the old days," she said. "He is one of ours."

Luther's heart nearly stopped. Did she mean they owned Buster? He knew the wild herds often included tame horses that had wandered off from farms or ranches. Is that what the old man was saying?

The young woman must have read his mind.

"No, no, I meant he is a Choctaw horse. My family brought many horses like him with us when we were forced to move here to Indian Territory. But there are not very many left that are like him. Grandfather says this horse of yours has the old blood, very pure old blood, blood of the original spirit dogs."

Before Luther could ask what a spirit dog was, the old man was talking again and motioning to them.

"Grandfather wants to show you something," she said. "He wants you to lead him out to our back pasture."

"You mean he wants to ride on Buster?" Luther asked in astonishment.

"Yes, we will have to help him."

It took both of them to lift her grandfather into the saddle, but after Luther had checked the cinch he looked up and saw that the old man suddenly seemed much younger and was sitting the horse easily and gracefully.

With Luther leading Buster from the left side and the granddaughter walking on the right side, they went down past the barn and followed a narrow footpath out toward a grassy meadow. Suddenly Buster made a sound, a low snuffling nicker, which Luther had never heard him make before. He looked over and realized the pony was on high alert. Then Luther heard a horse neigh and saw five horses, all different colors, but with the same size and body type as Buster, galloping right at them. They stopped just before the wire fence and milled about. Then one of the horses squealed and Buster tossed his head and gave a little prance. *Oh, glory,* thought Luther, and looked up at the old man, ready to pull him off if Buster started to act up. But the old man was smiling and chuckling and pointing at the horses, which Luther now realized were all mares.

The grandfather looked down at Luther and grinned.

"Hoke," he said, "Hoke," and spoke to his granddaughter in Choctaw.

"Amafo wanted you to see them so that you will know they are like a secret treasure for us," she explained.

Buster sure looks like he thinks they're a treasure, Luther thought.

IT WASN'T HARD TO GUESS what the old man had in mind for the young stallion. If it was true that these mares were among the very few survivors of the nearly pure Choctaw horse bloodlines and Buster was too, then they might want to use Buster to sire more like them.

Luther caught the young woman looking at him with an amused expression and he felt himself start to blush.

"We go back now," said the grandfather in unaccented English.

"Whew," sighed Luther as he quickly turned Buster away from the mares' pasture. He had feared for a moment that Buster was going to get overexcited about the mares and the old man would be bucked off and die.

They'd have probably shot Buster right there if that had happened, he thought.

Back at the house, as they eased the old man down from

the saddle, Luther felt him trembling. The grandfather suddenly seemed very shaky. Together Luther and the young woman carried him onto the porch and set him in a rocking chair and put a woolen blanket over his knees.

While Luther had been looking at the Choctaw mares, David and his father had hitched their mules to the wagon and several women had appeared and begun to load it with piles of blankets and pillows, and baskets of food and water. David helped his mother onto the seat next to his father and then jumped in the back. The young woman went back to her grandfather's side. Luther, not wanting to be left behind, said a quick goodbye to the young woman and to the old man, but the old man's head was on his chest and he was already snoring softly.

Meanwhile, Buster was not happy to see the mules going off without him and Luther had to speak sharply to him to make him stand still while he mounted. Will had taught him that he should never let the pony move off until he, the rider, was securely in the saddle. But once they were half way up the lane he urged Buster into a steady lope and they soon caught up to the wagon.

"Go on ahead," said David. "Tell Lucy we're on our way."

Luther leaned over the pony's neck and urged Buster into a gallop, his dark hair tangling with Buster's silver mane as they flew down the road. Joel met him as he came riding into the schoolyard.

"How's Lucy?" Luther asked as he swung down off Buster.

"The doc set her arm," Joel told him. "Miss Maisey had

Cecil and Rilly take the younger children down to the creek to play beforehand. Good thing, too, 'cause Lucy screamed just awful. But the Doc gave her something to help the pain and says the arm will heal just fine."

Miss Maisey spotted Luther and came out to speak to him. "I take it you and Buster fulfilled your mission, then," she asked.

"Yes," answered Luther. "Her ma and pa are bringing the wagon. They should be here soon."

"Well done, Luther, and well done to you, too," she said, turning to stroke Buster, who responded by rubbing his very sweaty head up and down on the front of her starched white blouse. Luther pulled him back in embarrassment, but Miss Maisey just smiled.

"Some horses seem to have a special spirit of adventure, don't they?" she said to Luther. "How lucky you are that he found you two boys to share those adventures with. I have a feeling you will have many more stories to tell about this pony that you named Buster, don't you?"

That night Miss Maisey could hardly wait to get to her room after supper and begin to write a new series of stories about the adventures of the Choctaw pony her students had saved.

Fourteen

Too Soon, Too Much

It was late April, and a long, hot summer lay just ahead. Miss Maisey's classroom was already almost empty of older children, who, by late spring, were needed to help on their family farms and ranches. Luther, Lucy, and Joel were the oldest in the room now and assumed all the tasks like getting water from the well and sweeping the schoolyard each day.

The schoolroom was hot and stuffy, so Miss Maisey had begun to teach outdoors around the big plank table where they also ate their lunches. Miss Maisey had plans to go back home to Massachusetts when school was over, and she was not sure she would ever see these children again. Her newspaper stories had become so popular back east that a publisher was urging her to write a book about teaching in Indian Territory. Also, a certain young man was urging her to start a new life as his wife. She was both sad at the thought of ending this stage of her life and excited about the future.

Of course the children had picked up on her emotions. Although they did not know why Miss Maisey seemed sad and distracted, they began to feel that way themselves and found it hard to focus on their lessons.

LUTHER AND CECIL HAD THEIR own reasons for feeling sad and distracted. The weekly letters they received from their mother were still full of cheerful stories of seeing the spring snow on the Colorado mountain peaks. The letters also still included intricate sketches of the wildflowers, prairie dogs, and coyotes she could see in the meadow beyond the big wide porch of the hospital. Their mother had always encouraged the boys to include drawings in the letters they wrote to her and with her guidance Luther was becoming quite an accomplished artist. Recently, however, she had stopped writing anything about coming home.

Then a few days ago, The Judge had told them they would be going to visit their mother at the sanitarium as soon as school was out. The long trip out to Colorado to see the big Rocky Mountains was exciting to think about, but The Judge had been very somber when he talked to them. Cecil had asked why their Mother couldn't come home to them, instead, but The Judge just shook his head.

"She's not getting better, boys," he said in his direct way, "the consumption is worse and she is too weak to travel. She wants to see you as soon as possible."

Later that night, after they had gone to bed, Luther heard Cecil crying.

"She's gonna' die isn't she?" he whimpered. "Just like Joel's mama did."

Luther went over and climbed into his brother's bed.

"We don't know for sure," he whispered. "Let's just hope for the best. We got to be brave for her," and he held Cecil close until he fell asleep.

Luther himself did not sleep well that night. *I'm too big to cry,* he thought, but the tears came anyway.

A FEW DAYS LATER LUTHER and Cecil found Will and The Judge leaning over the backyard fence and talking.

"It's a way to preserve some of our heritage," they overheard Will say.

The Judge and Will turned to the boys as they approached.

"I had sent word to Will to ask him to have Buster gelded while we were on our trip to Colorado," The Judge said, "but he has another idea. You tell it, Will."

"So, Luther," began Will, "you remember meeting Amafo, my grandfather, and my cousin Sarah, at Lucy's place?"

"Yes, sir," answered Luther. "The day Lucy broke her arm."

"And he took you to see his band of mares, didn't he?" continued Will.

"Um, hum," nodded Luther, who by that time figured he knew what this was all about.

"Well," Will said, "you know those mares are real special to us because they trace right back to the horses the Choctaw brought along the hard trail to the Indian Territory years ago. It was a terrible trip and many of our people and their horses died on the way. Then over the years of hard times not all of us were able to hold on to our horses or feed them. Sometimes, when things were really bad, our horses just got turned loose to fend for themselves and turned wild like some in that bunch Buster came from."

Will moved to the top porch step then and sat down, motioning to Cecil and Luther to join him.

"Amafo managed to keep some of his father's horses and he kept on breeding them. Now though, he doesn't anymore have a stallion to match with those mares of his. But when he saw Buster that day he knew he had found another one of our horses."

"You know I told you, Buster's as pure Choctaw as they come," Will continued. "So..."

And *here it comes,* thought Luther,

"...we need you to allow Buster to be a stud horse to our mares and help us save this breed of horses for our children and grandchildren to know and respect. Otherwise, these horses, like a lot of our history and traditions, could be lost forever."

Will was looking straight at Luther when he said that and there was a fierce determination in that look, as well as an earnest plea in his voice. It scared Luther because there was something here that Will obviously thought Luther should be able to understand, but he didn't understand it... not really, not real deeply, anyway.

After all, Buster was his pony, the one he had dreamed of, and named, the one he and Cecil had saved all by themselves just last fall. Yet Will and his family acted like they thought Buster belonged to them somehow. In fact, it almost seemed like they thought Buster belonged to all of the Choctaws and Chickasaws and who knows how many other tribes.

FIFTEEN

A HARD DECISION

⋄⋄⋄⋄⋄⋄⋄⋄⋄⋄⋄⋄⋄⋄⋄⋄⋄⋄⋄⋄⋄⋄⋄⋄⋄⋄

Luther felt like a little kid being asked to do something he plain wasn't old enough to do. It was like he was being given a peek into a whole other world, one he was supposed to care enough about to sacrifice his precious pony for, but that he himself could never be part of, because he wasn't Choctaw or Chickasaw or any other kind of Indian.

He looked up at The Judge for some clue as to what to do or say to Will, but The Judge had his back to them. Then he looked at Cecil for help, but Cecil was just staring at Will with his mouth dropped open.

I've only had my pony for half a year, Luther was thinking. *Why should I have to give him up now?*

With horror, he realized tears were running down his face right here in front of everybody.

Will, recognizing Luther's embarrassment, looked away and then stood up. Still facing away, he said

"In a couple weeks we'll be moving our livestock up to Blackjack Mountain for the summer and we'd like to take Buster with us. Think on it and let me know."

Then Will gave a nod to The Judge and quickly left. Beth's voice eventually broke the dead silence that followed.

"Time to get washed up you all," she called out from the kitchen window. "Supper's 'bout ready."

DINNER WAS EATEN IN SILENCE, as usual, and the boys joined The Judge on the porch afterwards, as usual. But the only thing The Judge said all evening long was,

"Some decisions are best made after a good night's sleep. You boys go on to bed now."

Shortly after they were in bed the brothers heard the creak of the front yard gate and looked out their bedroom window to watch The Judge walk down the dark dusty road. Soon all they could see was the glow of his cigar, and then not even that. When Cecil started to ask a question, Luther snapped at him.

"Just go to sleep and leave me alone."

Even when he heard Cecil sniffling Luther just turned his back and burrowed further into his pillow. *Not fair,* he whispered to himself. *It's just not fair.*

WHEN LUTHER AND CECIL RODE up to the schoolhouse the next morning they saw a new horse tied next to Lucy's old piebald. It was a handsome bay gelding with a star on his forehead and one white sock, and he was tacked out with a good saddle and bridle. The bay nickered at Buster and Buster nickered back. They tied Buster nearby, picked up a drinking water bucket and went to the well to fill it.

Lucy was there with the other bucket. Luther wasn't feeling very friendly and did not meet her eyes. Lucy tilted her head and said "Halito?" but Luther barely nodded hello back. Lucy hesitated, her lips pressed together, then turned abruptly and started back with her full bucket. Later, at lunchtime, Luther and Lucy both took their horses to the water trough and let them drink.

"You got a new horse," remarked Luther, who was feeling just a little bad about having been rude earlier.

"Not for me," said Lucy sharply. "He's for you."

"What are you talking about?" retorted Luther.

"You know what I'm talking about," Lucy said. "You and Cecil will need something to ride while Buster is doing his duty, that's part of the deal."

"I haven't agreed to any deal," said Luther angrily.

Lucy ignored him and kept on "…and you get your pick of Buster's first foals. That's what grandfather told Uncle Will last night. You are supposed to try this horse out today and see if you like him."

"Forget it," snapped Luther and he jerked hard at Buster's rope to take him away, but Buster just planted his feet and pulled back.

Luther just stood there in shock. He had taken out his anger on his beloved pony, just what Will had taught him he must never do if he was to gain the trust of his horse. He closed his eyes tight in a grimace of shame and suddenly Lucy's arms were around him.

"Please," she said, "please don't be angry. It won't be forever and you will be so proud when you see Buster's babies. This way the spirit of our ancestors will live on through those babies and then their babies, forever. You'll be able to tell your children and their children the story of how you and Buster helped our horses survive, and they will keep the story of your Buster and our mares alive forever."

LUTHER OPENED HIS EYES TO find Joel standing right at his elbow. "How 'bout we take the bay horse down the road aways, just you and me," urged Joel.

Luther stared down at his little friend for a long second then handed Buster's rope to Lucy and took the bay gelding from her. He helped Joel climb up on to the saddle, tightened the girth, and mounted behind him. They put the bay through its paces as they went down the road and speculated that the horse had to have been trained by Will.

"He seems to know what you want before you even know it," said Luther grudgingly. "Whose horse is this, anyways?"

"I think Will trained him for his cousin, Sarah," Joel answered. "He's her buggy horse, too."

"Oh yeah," said Luther. "I've seen her driving out with him and looking right smart."

"She won't need him up in the mountains this summer," Joel continued, "and she's going to have a baby in the fall, so that's why they're loaning him to you now."

"Whoa!" said Luther, who had suddenly realized that none of this was happening by chance. Not only had Will and Lucy's family been carefully planning every detail, but somehow Joel knew all about it, too.

"I just don't seem to have any darn choice in this," Luther complained to Joel. "That's what makes me mad. It just isn't fair."

"Let's go sit on the bridge at the creek," Joel suggested.

"You mean we're skipping school?" asked Luther.

"Exactly," said Joel, "Miss Maisey won't mind. School might as well be out anyway for all the work we're doing, and she's leaving town soon."

"You sure know a lot about everybody's business these days," Luther remarked after he and Joel had tied up the bay and gone to sit on the edge of the bridge.

"Yep, well, that's the thing about being me," Joel said.

"What do you mean?" asked Luther.

"Come on," said Joel, "you know most people think midgets like me are either idiots or some kind of windup toy. They talk about things in front of me that they wouldn't in front of you 'cause they half the time don't notice I'm even there, so long as I keep quiet. Miss Maisey and my Dad know I want to be scientist or a doctor, but anybody else would laugh at the idea."

"You never told me that!" exclaimed Luther, feeling that he should have known this already.

"Well, I do. I want to know why there are little people like me," Joel said. "I want to find out what goes wrong to make us like this. It's just my body, not my mind that's different."

"Well, you're the smartest person I know," stated Luther. "I think you're even smarter than The Judge."

"Well thanks," said Joel with a wry smile. Then the smile faded as he turned to Luther and said "I know about your mother."

"What, how?" said Luther. He felt like the ground had just shifted under him.

"You know my Mom died at the same sanitarium and she had the consumption, too, although now the doctors are calling it tuberculosis," Joel said.

Luther nodded.

"Well, your Dad, The Judge, he comes over after dinner sometimes and he and my Dad talk. Not just about our mothers and us, but about lots of things like the future of the Indian Territory and whether it will become part of a new State of Oklahoma or form a state of its own. I can hear everything they say 'cause my bed is up against the window. So I also know that it's not just losing Buster that you're afraid of, it's about maybe losing your Mother, too, …and no, it's not fair, none of it."

SIXTEEN

THE WAY FORWARD

◇◇◇◇◇◇◇◇◇◇◇◇◇◇◇◇◇◇◇◇◇◇◇◇◇◇◇◇◇◇◇◇◇◇◇◇◇◇◇

*J*oel stood up and leaned against the guardrail of the bridge. He took a deep breath before he spoke again.

"It took me a long time to forgive my Mom for going off and dying. I kept thinking it's not fair. I needed her and she left me. It's not fair that your mother might die, either. But they neither one had any choice, you see, not against that disease. It's another reason I want to be a doctor, to find cures for diseases like that. It's also unfair that Will asked you to give up Buster when your pony dreams have only just come true and your ma is so sick."

"Stop!" said Luther. "I decided I'm doing it."

"You are?" asked Joel, turning back to look at his friend.

"Yeah, it was something Lucy said, and how she said it. I just needed to understand how big a thing this is for them. Maybe Cecil and me were supposed to save Buster just for this reason. Maybe he really is a spirit horse from the past. I don't know. It just seems right, I guess, to let him help save his own kind, to help them survive."

"Well," said Joel, "I think The Judge and your mom will be proud of you for that decision. Makes me proud to know you, too," he said with his lopsided grin.

"Jeez, Joel," Luther laughed, "sometimes you sound just like Miss Maisey."

"Nothing wrong with that," said Joel. "But you gotta know she's breaking my heart by leaving."

"You and Miss Maisey?" exclaimed an astounded Luther.

"Yes," said Joel, in a firm voice, "and I plumb told her so, too, and she has promised to write to me every month for as long as I write her back and tell her everything that's going on with everyone here. She even knows somebody that will be a big help when I'm ready to leave for college...so there!"

Luther just shook his head, which was reeling anyway with all these mighty decisions and disturbing revelations. As they rode back Luther had the feeling his world had suddenly gotten a lot bigger and wider than he had thought it was, and scarier, too. Joel seemed so grown up back there.

I'm being pushed hard to grow up, too, he realized.

IN BED THAT NIGHT LUTHER tried to quiet his mind and organize his thoughts. That his mother was probably dying was one thought. He imagined writing that out and laying it down on a table. He pictured that thought being written on purple paper with a black border because it was a dark thought about a life ending. It made him dread the trip to see her because it might be the last time he would, but on the other hand he needed to see her so he could remember her better, especially her voice, and her eyes.

His next thought was that *Cecil's going to need me; he's not going to understand.*

He put that thought on the imaginary table, too, written

on grey paper; grey paper because it was also a dark thought. But then he added a saucy little scalloped edge to the grey paper *because Cecil's such a happy person inside,* he was thinking, *What's that word Miss Maisey had said about him? Oh yeah, 'ebullient'. She called Cecil an 'ebullient being. His being so happy inside helps me,* Luther reflected, *'cause he makes me laugh, keeps me from being too serious about things.*

Luther turned over in bed and pondered some more.

Miss Maisey called me "a deep and steady soul," whatever that means. I guess brothers like us kind of balance each other out and so maybe we can get through all this if we just stick together.

Luther then imagined writing that thought down on grass green paper because green is about life and growing.

Luther's final thought was about Buster and how he would be with the mares, doing what stud horses do; making babies, protecting his herd, running free up in the mountains…forgetting all about him!

He suddenly realized he was just plain jealous. Lucy and his other Choctaw friends would be up there enjoying all that and he wouldn't be. He imagined putting that thought on green paper, too, but this was a dark muddy green, the green of envy.

OK, so how do I deal with that ugly thought? he asked himself.

Then Luther had what Miss Maisey called an 'epiphany.'

Why shouldn't I go up to Blackjack Mountain, too? he wondered. *Would they let me come after we get back from Colorado? Could I do the trip on my own on the bay horse? Heck, the bay probably already knows the way and he's big enough to carry Cecil and provisions, too, and I couldn't not take Cecil.*

Would we be in the way? Maybe they could use the extra hands, and the extra horse, too. Luther's thoughts were now running so fast he couldn't have written them down even in his head. He was so excited he hauled off and pounded his pillow with his fist and shouted. "By gum, we're gonna do it!"

The noise woke Cecil. He turned over to peer at his brother and saw he was sitting up in bed, his eyes shining, his cheeks burning, and he had his jaw set in that familiar determined way. *Oh boy, oh boy,* Cecil thought gleefully, *we're starting another adventure!*

Then the little boy turned back over and fell asleep again. Soon Cecil began to dream a beautiful dream about seeing flowers blooming in snow from a train window and sleeping rough on a bed of crinkly dry leaves somewhere deep in some woods and laughing with his mother. Or maybe it was the gurgle and splash of a mountain stream that sounded like her laughter, or maybe it was both. The best dreams are like that and sometimes they even come true.

Seventeen

A Promise

◇◇

*A*trickle of sweat rolled down Luther's forehead and dripped onto his nose. The little bunch of wild flowers he had picked on the way to the cemetery had already wilted in the heat. The grave was mounded with bare dirt. The engraved headstone was still lying next to the grave, waiting to be set into the hard baked ground.

"What are we 'sposed to say to her?" asked Cecil, who was leaning against him.

"I guess just what you would say if she was alive," answered Luther.

Cecil thought a minute, grinned, and said "Hey, Ma, we're going up to Blackjack Mountain!" Then he glanced up at Luther with a worried frown. "Is it ok to feel happy?" he asked Luther.

"Well," said Luther "she was pretty clear when she told us she didn't want us to be sad. So I think it's alright." Then he put his arm around his little brother and gave him a quick hug.

As he leaned over to place the flowers on top of the dirt, Luther had to press his lips tightly together, though, because he could not help feeling sad.

Ma had always wanted to hear every detail about every little adventure we had, he was thinking. *She always listened to our stories and laughed at our dumb jokes and told me she read my letters over and over again and showed my drawings to all her friends.*

Silently he made a solemn pledge.

I promise, Ma. I promise I'll report to you on everything that happens, every single thing, and even draw you pictures like you always taught me to do.

And so he did.

EIGHTEEN

LETTERS FROM BLACKJACK MOUNTAIN

Dear Ma,

Well, it took us two whole days to get up to Lucy's family's camp on Blackjack Mountain. By us I mean me, Cecil, and Joel. Yes, Joel came, too. He said he wasn't gonna miss out and his Dad got him a little red molly mule to ride. The Judge and Joel's Dad borrowed a pack mule from Amos Lee's string, too, cause they said we needed to make sure we were bringing enough rations and stuff for us and plenty extra to share out so we wouldn't be a burden to anyone. They gave us a goodly talking to before we left, too, about what to expect to see up there. The Judge said a lot of the old folks, the elders, are really poor and poorly and being white boys we was going to get some unfriendly attention maybe. This is because of the times with all the Indians being judged whether they're real true Indians or not and about the whole Territory going to be divided up and then maybe going to be a part of a new State of Oklahoma. Joel's Dad he said there's lot of bad feelings and just plain worries going around and we might hear a lot of arguments about it, but if we stick close to Lucy's family we'd be ok. The Judge he said just be respectful and polite and look for ways to help out all the time.

To get up there we followed the Kiamichi River up to the foot of the mountain. Then we branched off to the east and then up a long steep trail that Will had described. It weren't hard to find as lots of people had been goin' up and down it looked like and we found the mark on the tree that Will said to look for. The gelding Will had loaned us seemed to recognize it, too, and just went right on up it at a right lively pace. Pretty soon we were spotting a few camps back in the woods, especially when we were near a stream and saw even a few cabins and lots of rough shelters. We mostly just got nods from anyone we met, but no one seemed surprised to see us. Of course later we found out they all knew we were coming.

We were pretty tired and getting a little worried we might have missed Lucy's family camp before we caught sight of Ida Mae running down the trail and yipping like a coyote. That was a mighty welcome sight I tell you. Next thing we know she's up behind Joel on his molly mule and pointing out a trail up on the right hand side which led us into a big open space with one big cabin and lots of log shelters of different sizes all around the edges and a view across the mountains. So now we're bedded down under one of the bigger shelters with a bunch of Lucy's cousins and some of them I know from school. They showed us how to hang our provisions from a tree so's the bears won't get to them, but there's so many dogs runnin' around in the camp it seems like we will know it if a bear comes close. At least I hope so.

Well I'll close this letter now cause it's getting too dark to write.

Your loving son

Luther.

Here's what the cabin looks like.

Dear Ma,

Guess what? Will and Beth is getting married. Lucy says they already did it at church, but that means something different. They're gonna have a real Choctaw wedding up here on the mountain. Lucy is all excited but Cecil and I are just plain surprised. I bet the Judge is gonna be surprised, too. I wonder if this means Beth won't be housekeeping for us anymore. That makes me sad to think about. Her biscuits are the best. And we like her a lot, too. We haven't seen her up here yet. Ida Mae says she's still working down in town. Another thing I haven't seen yet is Buster. I only caught sight of Will for a minute yesterday. We've been helping cutting and bringing in wood for the cooking fires. He just waved when he saw us and went on.

When we're not helping out, or hunting, or fishing, the boys all play stickball. At school we got left out of that when the Choctaw boys played it, but it always looked like fun. They call it ishtaboli. *But today we all got handed sticks, even Joel got him little kids size ones which made him laugh. These are called* kapucha *and the ball is called* towa. *So now we're learning how to play a little.*

Your loving son,

Luther

This is what Cecil's kapucha *(stickball sticks) look like*

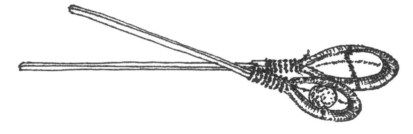

Dear Ma,

We've been up on Blackjack Mountain for almost two weeks now. Your probably wondering what we do all day. Well, Cecil spends most of his time trying to learn to play ishtaboli. He comes back ever day all bruised and sore and just grinning and laughing and when he's not playing he's busy learning how to make his own kapucha. He is really growing fast and is taller and bigger than I am already, even though he's that much younger. I guess I take after the Judge more in size and Cecil takes after your kinfolks. Maybe my growth spurt will come later like Miss Maisey suggested or maybe I'll just have to be satisfied with not being a tall man.

Anyways, I spend most of my time with Lucy's cousins that are near my age and we get ordered around a lot by the aunties who have us doing all sorts of chores from getting wood gathered in, working the garden patches, getting water from the creek, picking berries and hunting squirrels and rabbits. Some of the men have guns and they bring in the venison and sometime a turkey and we have a lot of good stew.

All the elders here want us to learn how to do things the old fashioned way of the Choctaws. When I tried to get a rabbit with my slingshot and kept missing, one of the old uncles brought me this piece of carved wood called a rabbit stick only it looks more like a club, and showed me how to use it to knock down a rabbit. Instead of throwing it directly at the rabbit you do it sideways and catch the rabbit as it moves. I'm getting the hang of it now. I think he called the stick an iti nipa. I know iti *means wood or made of wood, but I will have to ask about the rest. Of course I hadn't never skinned a rabbit either, but one of the aunties showed me how and then said, ok now you are rabbit skinner and all the aunties started laughing. I didn't exactly want to have that name, but sometimes Ida Mae comes and gets me and tells me the aunties need me to do it. Since they do all the cooking and feeding I guess it's only fair. Now Joel, he hangs around the aunties and the old men all the time and says he is doing it to learn Choctaw and Chickasaw. We're all picking it up pretty fast, but Joel is understanding the jokes, too, and that's something I can't do yet. The aunties let Joel come along on his molly mule when they go to gather herbs and stuff for their medicines. He says he wants to know all the secrets they have about healing and that there is something in the old beliefs about little people like him and these herb medicines.*

Joel also listens in on all the talk about the government doing the enrollments and allotments and reports back to us. The whole thing is pretty confusing, but it seems to be something that most of the elders don't want or trust the whites about. But some of the younger men, especially some of the mixed blood ones, seem to think it is going to happen no matter what because the government wants it so they better make the best of it. There's lot of discussions around the campfires every night about this, like Pa warned us about.

Did you know people like us are called intruders? One of the older boys from another camp called me that and not in a nice way. I know we're called Na Hullo, but I didn't realize all what that could mean. I've got lots of questions about all this I'm saving up to talk over with The Judge when we get back. I don't know if we're supposed to apologize for living in the Territory or not. Sometimes it seems that way, but we're treated just like part of Lucy's and Will's family here in our camp.

Well, it's getting dark so I have to stop writing.

Your loving son,

Luther

PS This is what my rabbit hunting stick looks like.

Dear Ma,

Will and Beth are getting married the Choctaw way in a few days and it looks like we are expecting lots of visitors to come up the mountain for that. The aunties are working us hard to get the camp ready. Almost feels like the circus is coming to town there's so much excitement.

One thing makes me sad is I don't get to talk to Lucy as much as we use to at school. She's growing tall and getting real pretty too, but she and Rilly and the other girls are always really busy with women's work and taking care of the littlest kids and stuff. I also saw her working on a basket the other day with some of the older aunties who weave those cane baskets all the time. I know they can get cash money for the prettiest ones. Ida Mae said Lucy's saving up for something special she wants to go to but she wouldn't say what that is.

I finally did see Will long enough to talk and he promised that after the wedding he'll take me over to where Buster has led his mares to. So that's something. I can't hardly wait to see him.

Your loving son,

Luther

Here's how the basket makers weave their baskets.

Dear Ma,

It's a good thing The Judge and Joel's Pa showed up for the wedding else I wouldn't have enough paper left to write on. Now I know you want ever detail, but I tell you it was hard to figure out all what was happening. First of all, I don't know where everyone got their fancy dress from, but most of the men had on shirts with ribbon trimming on them and same with the women who wore bright colors and white aprons. The aunties as usual ran the whole show near about. They sat Beth down on the ground and put a piece of cotton on her head and then everybody started heaping up all kinds of things on her like beads and flowers and things wrapped in leather and cloth and I don't know what else until she was about covered with stuff. Then she suddenly got up and spilled it all on the ground and started running away. Joel said maybe she changed her mind, but everyone started whooping and yelling and here come Will hightailing it after her. Beth gave him a good run but he finally caught her and brought her back all breathless and laughing so I guess it was all in fun after all. Then they stood in front of the cabin with all the old folks around, even Will's grandpa who I don't know how they got him all the way up here, was in his rocking chair up on the porch. Then one of the elders stepped up who Joel said later he found out was an old chief of the Choctaws. He commenced to giving a pretty long talk to Will and Beth that sometimes sounded like he was preaching and sometimes like he was telling a story, but he finally said something that seemed to make it official and everybody got to talking and the food got put out and it was a real feast, I tell you. Later on the drums came out and there was stomp dancing and singing the Choctaw way and it went on and on into the night around the campfires. I was worried we should have given something to Beth, too, but The Judge said he had already given something to Beth and Will from us. I think I'll make something special anyway and give it to them just from me and Cecil 'cause they both of them have taken good care of us in different ways.

Your loving son,

Luther

The ribbons and stuff everyone had on their shirts looked like this.

Dear Ma,

So a few days ago Will sent a message saying for me to pack my bedroll and some provisions and borrow a horse and be saddled up and ready to ride out before dawn the next day. I can tell you this was more exciting than any wedding. First we rode up to where a fast flowing spring comes out of the ground and flows down to make the creek and Will said the water goes all the way down to the Kiamichi eventually. He said this water was known to heal all kinds of ills and hurts. He showed me a big sundial on a rock he said the Choctaw had put there when they discovered this medicine spring water. The water tasted like metal sort of and was icy cold and there was this orange stuff all around the ground there that Will said was minerals that settle out from the water. There was a place down below where it had been dammed up to make a soaking place and Will and I had a good soak although it was so cold I could hardly feel anything when we got out and my skin was all puckered up. My clothes were all hot from the sun and it felt good to put them back on I tell you.

We rode on following trails that Will said were made by deer and hunters and people who lived at least part of the year up here. But sometimes a trail would end up in brush so thick we had to turn back and find another way through. Finally we came to a place above a creek where Will said there was a natural salt lick and sure enough there was fresh horse sign and tracks all around there as well as deer sign. We tied our horses there and went on by foot cause Will said he figured Buster and his mares were up ahead in what he called the burn. That's where a lightning strike had started a forest fire years ago and so the grass could grow good and thick there.

Will told me to follow him and do what he did and that meant trying not to snap branches or shuffle my feet. Then he squatted down and pointed to the right. It's funny how you think it's always dead quiet in the woods, but that's not so. When your really still and listening there's all kinds of noises from insects and frogs and birds and the breeze rustlin' in the leaves and such and all of a sudden I was also hearing munching sounds and hoof falls and that it was horses grazing right nearby. Will didn't move for the longest time and I was getting impatient and then I wondered how come Will thinks this is Buster's herd anyway? I knowed there were lots of other folks horses turned out up there. Later on he told me he knows the different shapes of the hoofs of each mare and that I should memorize exactly what Buster's hoof prints look like and how they grow and change from time to time so I could always track him.

Well, finally Will signals me to stand up slow and now I can see Buster and he sees us. Without thinking I start right to him calling to him and all of sudden he's got his mares pulled up close behind him and he's standin' there facing me dead on with his head way up and he makes this really loud chuffing sound I'd never heard before and stamps his hooves. I was so surprised I stepped right back and bumped into Will who was grinnin' at me. "Well, you got yourself a real stallion now," he said.

Actually what bothered me was I didn't know if I had a horse at all. This wasn't the Buster I knew. But Will said just give him some time and keep talkin' and he'll remember you. So I leaned up against an oak tree and commenced a one-sided conversation with Buster while Will went back and got our saddle horses and started to make us a camp nearby. I had brought a little corn in my pocket, too, and when Buster finally came close enough I reached out my hand and offered it and he come right to me and let me rub his forehead the way he always liked. Then I whispered in his ear and called him by his spirit name. He put his head over my shoulder and let me hug him.

We stayed up there with the little herd through the next morning until Buster and the mares moved off into the woods and then we rode back to Lucy's family camp. We just let our horses have their heads and take us there 'cause they seemed to know the best way down.

I been thinking ever since what all this means about Buster being a herd stallion and such and seeming so happy and free up there. My feelings are all mixed up. Will says there's a Choctaw word, Apookta, that means place of happiness. I'm guessing this is Apookta for Buster.

Your loving son,

Luther.

P.S. Now I'm writing by moonlight. It's a full moon night and almost bright as day. I can see bats flying and saw a big owl drift down and float across the camp and we heard a fox scream awhile ago. That's a sound makes your neck hairs stand up I tell you.

Here's what the camp looks like in the moonlight.

Dear Ma,

We packed up the camp last week and went down as far as the river where we stayed a couple of days because there was a stickball game to be played in a cleared area along the river there. It was something to see and it went on and on for most of two days with hardly any rules I could make out, although Cecil and Joel says there are some. The playing was really rough and fast and Cecil got mowed down a few times, but he stayed right in there and made me proud. Everybody just seemed to have fun and there seemed to be a lot of visiting going on between the people who had come to see and lots of cheering and eating and lots of maybe good natured teasing and catcalls. Then later there was dancing and singing.

I did get a chance to visit awhile with Lucy and Ida Mae though. But I found out something that really has me kind of upset. When I said to Lucy I guessed I would see her at school soon she said no, I won't be there. Ida Mae chipped in and said Lucy's going to boarding school to be a teacher lady like Miss Maisey. My mouth must have been hanging open and I didn't know what to say. I guess I should be happy for her, like I should be happy for Buster for growing up into a herd stallion, and even like I should happy that you are in heaven, Ma, and not sick anymore, but I feel like my whole world is changing and I am being left behind.

Your loving son,

Luther

Here's what the ishtaboli game looked like. Cecil's the one on the left.

NJNETEEN

THE BUGGY RIDE
1904

◇◇

*T*wo years had passed since Luther, Cecil, and Joel had spent the summer up on Blackjack Mountain. Luther was now almost fifteen and he had grown and filled out and was looking forward to a good paying job on the railroad the next summer, and then enrolling at the Oklahoma A and M preparatory college next fall.

Cecil was continuing to grow taller and bigger and was turning out to be a star baseball player, and already writing sports stories for the local newspaper. Joel, of course, had long ago grown as tall as he would ever be. He was planning to spend the summer in Paris, Texas, assisting Dr. Rumsfeld at the hospital there. After that, he would be going to Boston, Massachusetts, to live with Miss Maisey and her husband and go to a private school that would prepare him for college.

It was coming on Easter and Luther was looking forward to seeing Lucy again. She had spent the Christmas break at the home of friends she had made at her academy, and so it had been awhile since he had seen her. They had been writing to each other ever since Lucy had gone away to boarding school, though, and he thought they knew pretty much everything the other was doing and thinking.

Buster would be turned back out with his mares soon after Luther left for his summer job and Will had said he would take care of him while Luther was away. Luther had earned good money working cattle for the local ranchers with Buster who was turning out to be one smart cowpony.

Buster had also been allowed to stay a stallion. When they came back after that first summer on Blackjack Mountain The Judge was talked into allowing a trial period where Buster could prove he could behave himself around other horses if he stayed a stallion. The pony's natural traits of kindness, intelligence, and willingness had come through, and he had shown himself to be a gentleman wherever he was ridden. By now he was the sire of four yearlings and three foals already born this year, with two of the other mares expected to foal next month.

Meanwhile, Luther had decided Buster needed to make himself even more useful by learning to pull a buggy. Under Will's direction, Luther got him used to the long reins again and then to dragging a log around behind him, which at first he did not at all appreciate, but had soon got used to. Then he was doubled up with an experienced buggy horse to get the hang of pulling the buggy and responding to a driver rather than a rider. Finally, Buster was harnessed and put in the traces of the Judge's buggy. He seemed to enjoy prancing downtown and showing off his smooth pacing gates.

Luther had been hatching a plan and had saved up enough from work to buy a small second-hand buggy of his own. He repaired it and painted it white and got their neighbor, Mrs. Sellars, to make some cushions for it from some pretty printed feed sacks. With Buster's strawberry roan coloring, white socks and long silvery mane and tail, they made quite a flashy sight as they drove around town.

One afternoon a couple of Miz Palmer's lady helpers waved Luther down and asked for a buggy ride. They looked mighty pretty in the little white buggy with their flouncy dresses and colored parasols and they giggled and flirted with Luther until he was red in the face. Quite a few of the townspeople people noticed the fuss. When Luther stopped in front of Miz Palmer's and helped the young women step down from the buggy, he got a quick kiss on the cheek from one of them. It did not take long for that scene to be reported to The Judge by one of his law clerks.

That night the Judge suggested a walk after dinner, just he and Luther. That turned out to be the first real man-to-man talk Luther and the Judge had ever had. The Judge talked about his courtship of Luther's Ma and how she would not have considered him if he had had a poor reputation as to his relationships with other women. He gently gave Luther some facts of life and love, which Luther had given very little thought to before. After that the Judge offered him whiskey from his pocket flask and a cigar. Smoking the cigar turned out to be the worst part of the evening and made Luther vow never to touch one again.

Being told to stay home while The Judge and Luther took their walk had not set well with Cecil, of course, but he got some satisfaction later from seeing the aftermath of his brother's whiskey and cigar initiation. Of course after

Luther had puked it all out, Cecil relented and brought him a basin of water and a clean rag.

If that's what happens when you grow up, I'll just stay a kid, thought Cecil, as he listened to his brother moaning.

A FEW WEEKS LATER LUTHER had the little buggy dusted off, the harness and brass all polished up and had even given Buster a bath. Lucy was to come to church on Easter Sunday and he wanted to be ready. Now Lucy, at fifteen, was already a rare beauty, and that Sunday she was dressed in her school finery with a long sleeved high necked white blouse and full skirt with all the ruffles, a band of blue velvet around her neck, white lace gloves and a flowered bonnet pinned at a jaunty angle on her upswept hairdo.

Luther, dressed in his only suit and tie, his dark hair parted in the middle and smoothed down with pomade, was looking pretty fine himself. He didn't even feel shy going up to Lucy after church and asking her if she'd like to take a buggy ride.

Lucy was willing. She had spotted Buster and admired the buggy earlier, and secretly hoped that Luther was going to ask. This did not stop her big brother, David, from checking that Buster was harnessed correctly and that the buggy was sound before he gave the go ahead, but he nodded his approval with a twinkle in his eye.

TO SAY THAT LUTHER WAS feeling very proud and happy as they trotted down the road, with his beloved Buster in the harness in front and Lucy sitting next to him, would be an understatement. In fact, Luther felt so happy that he decided at the last minute that he would extend the ride by taking the track across the creek and back around to the new part of town where brick buildings were now being built. The only thing he had forgotten to take into account was the fact that every time he had ridden Buster across the creek in the past he had let him jump across from one bank to the other, instead of wading across at the graveled ford.

As they approached the ford Buster pricked up his ears and quickened his pace, and if Luther had been paying attention to driving, instead of talking and laughing with Lucy, he might have avoided the crash. But he wasn't, and he didn't.

When Buster reached the creek bank he gathered his hindquarters up under him and took a mighty leap right across the ford. As he landed on the opposite bank the buggy followed him only as far as the creek bed where it hit hard and toppled over. Lucy in her lovely white outfit landed on her bottom about waist deep in the muddy water while Luther hung onto the side of the buggy all tangled in the reins and shafts and half drowned. Buster was confused about being restrained by the buggy wreck, but being a wise horse he chose to just stand still and wait to be released.

TWENTY

APOOKTA

◇◇◇◇◇◇◇◇◇◇◇◇◇◇◇◇◇◇◇◇◇◇◇◇◇◇◇◇◇◇◇◇◇◇◇◇◇◇

*L*ater, as Buster carried two ominously silent young people, who were dripping cold water and itchy mud all over his bare back, the pony realized he was on the road to Lucy's house. At that point we might speculate that Buster would be remembering the first time he had made that trip to Lucy's place. After all, that was the day she had broken her arm and the day he had so bravely saved Luther from the rattlesnake by killing it dead.

But no, Buster, you see, was thinking only about his little band of mares and foals waiting for him just up ahead at the Thurman's farm. Of course we know that Buster, like all Choctaw horses, was a kind and gentle animal and able and willing to carry and pull and pack and plow whenever his people needed him to. But we also know that horses have their own needs and dreams, and their very own definition of happiness. As for Buster, true happiness, Apookta, would always mean the freedom to live with his mares and foals, much as he had done up on Blackjack Mountain, and thus keep the powerful spirit of his ancestors alive.

When Buster turned in at the Thurman's gate that evening, it was already getting dark. By that time he was so eager to join his herd that he switched into his fast pacing gait. To stay on his pony riding bareback at this fast pace Luther had to sit deeper and lean back a bit. Lucy, in turn, had to grab Luther around the waist, put her head up against his back, and hold on tight. This caused both of them to finally smile a little secret smile.

As for Buster, these weight shifts were so helpful in balancing the double burden of two riders' weight that he was able to stretch out and move even faster. In fact, he was moving so swiftly and smoothly now that it almost seemed as if they were flying above the ground. At just that moment the very last rays of sunlight lit Buster's tail, making it look as if a fountain of silver was streaming out behind them. And then they were gone.

EPILOGUE

INTO THE FUTURE

◇◇◇◇◇◇◇◇◇◇◇◇◇◇◇◇◇◇◇◇◇◇◇◇◇◇◇◇◇◇◇◇◇◇◇◇

*W*e leave this story now; with Lucy, Luther, Joel, Cecil, and Ida Mae growing up and following different paths to their adult lives. We can be sure that these friends stayed in touch with each other by writing letters, because that was the way folks communicated back then. Unfortunately, none of these later letters have been found, so we can only guess what the future might have held for each of them and for their families. We can also be sure that Buster and his offspring would have continued to be cherished by Will and Lucy's family and would never be forgotten by Luther.

It has been more than a century since Luther dreamed a pony, woke a spirit, and made a personal sacrifice. Luther chose to help perpetuate a rare strain of horses with unique equine characteristics and significant cultural heritage and historical importance.

In the same spirit that moved Luther to make the right decision, there are people in our own times who have chosen to help sustain and protect these heritage horses for the generations to come. May that spirit reach out to you and to yours as well.

THE END

Choctaw Words Glossary

◇◇◇◇◇◇◇◇◇◇◇◇◇◇◇◇◇◇◇◇◇◇◇◇◇◇◇◇◇◇◇◇◇◇

Halito: *Hello*

Yakoke: *Thank You*

Na Hullo: *White/European*

Amafo: *My grandfather*

Ishtaboli: *The traditional game of stickball**

Kapucha: *Ishtaboli stick*

Towa: *Ball*

Iti nipa: *Rabbit stick*

*Ishtaboli Video:

https://www.youtube.com/watch?v=SOFPg6Da-Aw

Informational Links

For further information please follow these internet links:

www.thespiritofblackjackmountain.com

http://www.thespiritofblackjackmountain.com/articles–history.html

http://www.choctawnationculture.com/default.aspx

http://www.choctaw.org/culture/ihinoshi.html

http://www.red-road-farm.com/choctaw2.html

http://www.centerforamericasfirsthorse.org/

http://www.archives.gov/education/lessons/fed-indian-policy/

http://www.livestockconservancy.org/

http://www.frankhopkins.com/mustangform.html

http://www.southwestspanishmustangassociation.com/

Also:

Choctaw County Historical Society and Museum

307 North B Street P.O. Box 577. Hugo, OK 74743

www.friscodepot.org/society.html

Pushmataha County Historical Society and Museum

119 W Main St, Antlers, OK 74523

Oklahoma Historical Society's

Chronicles of Oklahoma

http://digital.library.okstate.edu/Chronicles/index.html

Selected Bibliography

Carson, James Taylor. "Horses and the Economy and Culture of the Choctaw Indians, 1690-1840," in *Ethnohistory* 42, no.3 (1995) 495-513.

Cobb, Amanda J. *Listening to Our Grandmothers' Stories: The Bloomfield Academy for Chickasaw Females, 1852-1949.* Lincoln: University of Nebraska Press, 1992.

Debo, Angie. *The Rise and Fall of the Choctaw Republic.* Norman: University of Oklahoma Press, 1934

Debo, Angie. *And Still the Waters Run: The Betrayal of the Five Civilized Tribes.* Princeton: Princeton University Press, 1940.

Debo, Angie. *Prairie City: the story of an American community.* New York: Knopf, 1944.

Kidwell, Clara Sue. *The Choctaws in Oklahoma: From Tribe to Nation, 1855-1970.* Norman: University of Oklahoma Press, 2007.

Mould, Tom. *Choctaw Tales.* Jackson: University Press of Mississippi, 2004.

Mowdy-Bond, Carol. *Oklahoma's Historical Little Dixie*, San Antonio: HPN Books/Lammert Publishing, 2015

St. Jean, Wendy. *Remaining Chickasaw in Indian Territory, 1830s-1907.* Tuscaloosa: The University of Alabama Press, 2011.

Sawyer, Sarah Elisabeth, Ed. *Touch My Tears: Tales from the Trail of Tears.* Canton, TX: RockHaven Publishing, 2013.

Sponenberg, D. Phillip. *The Choctaw Horse.* Accessed at http://www.choctawnation.com/history/choctaw-nation-history.

Spring, Joel. *The Cultural Transformation of a Native American Family and Its Tribe, 1763-1995; A Basket of Apples.* Mahwah, N.J.: Lawrence Erlbaum Associates, 1996.

Tingle, Tim. *Walking the Choctaw Road.* El Paso:Cinco Punto Press, 2003

Discussion and Research Questions for Readers

◇◇◇◇◇◇◇◇◇◇◇◇◇◇◇◇◇◇◇◇◇◇◇◇◇◇◇◇◇◇◇◇◇◇◇◇◇

1. Is there any difference between a cyclone and a tornado? What causes a tornado? Can a tornado really pick up part of a building and move it somewhere else?

2. What does a Barred Plymouth Rock chicken look like? What about a Jersey milk cow? Why were these types of farm animals popular with frontier homesteaders?

3. Where does the Red River start and where does it flow to? What kind of boats would have carried supplies up and down the river in 1900?

4. Looking at a map can you find the train tracks that linked Paris, Texas to Monet, Missouri ? Find five towns in Oklahoma that were built along that rail line. Do any of those towns still have their railroad depot buildings? Do any trains still run on these tracks?

5. Where did the Choctaw and Chickasaw people live before they were forced to move to Indian Territory? When were they moved there and why?

6. In what year did Oklahoma become a state? Is there still a Choctaw Nation or a Chickasaw Nation? What is the legal difference today between the State of Oklahoma and the Choctaw Nation or the Chickasaw Nation?

7. Tuberculosis was called consumption in the early days. When was a medicine that could cure this terrible disease invented? Is tuberculosis still a dangerous disease? What are the symptoms, how do you catch it, and how is it treated today?

8. Can you find a picture of a Choctaw pony, or any Colonial Spanish Mustang, on the internet? Why are these horses so important in American history? Were there horses in our country before the Spanish explorers came in the 1500s?

9. Joel was interested in finding out the scientific or medical reason why there are little people like him. What has scientific research discovered about dwarfism since then that would answer Joel's question?

10. Can you find Blackjack Mountain and the Kiamichi River on a map of Oklahoma?

11. Is stickball still played today? Why was it called "The Little Brother of War?" What does this tell us about how Choctaw disputes were often settled through discussion and competitive games instead of by killing each other in wars?

12. What is a "horse whisperer"? Do you think Will was one of these? Why do you think his methods of horse training are so popular today?

13. Where would Lucy have gone to boarding school in 1900? What would a school like that have been like and what subjects would she have studied?

14. Can you find a picture of a one room school house? Are there any one room school houses still being used anywhere in the United States? Do you think it helped the younger children to be learning in the same room as the older kids? Do you think the older kids learned from helping teach the younger ones?

15. Would you have liked to have had a teacher like Miss Maisey? Why do you think the students respected and behaved well for her?

16. Can you find a picture of the horses the Spanish explorers brought to America?

16. Pick one or more of the characters in this book and write a story about what might have happened to them after our story ended. Make it authentic for the times in which they lived.

17. What do you think might have been the secret "spirit name" Luther gave to Buster?

About the Author

SARAH SILVER grew up on a horse and cattle farm in the foot-hills of Virginia's Blue Ridge Mountains. Her career has been focused on rural community education and non-profit youth development programs. She worked for more than two decades in southwestern Colorado where she enjoyed exploring high mountain trails on her own beloved cowpony, Peggy Sue.

A life-long advocate for equitable access to higher education, Sarah teaches for her alma mater, Prescott College, and serves her southern Oregon community as a college and career counselor and mentor. Dream a Pony / Wake a Spirit is her first novel.

ABOUT THE ILLUSTRATOR

"AN ARTIST BY TRADE, AN educator by choice," sums up Paul King. A native Oklahoman who feels there is no better place to create his art, Paul has always expressed himself through visual images in a variety of mediums. Retiring after thirty six years as a CareerTech educator, King has returned to his passion of being an artist, while maintaining his sense of responsibility to the community.

As a proud Oklahoma Choctaw, his artwork depicts his culture and family heritage. Observing the Spanish mustangs in southeastern Oklahoma has motivated King to bring awareness to their birthright. Through Dream a Pony / Wake a Spirit, it is his desire that funding will continue the preservation of these historic Choctaw ponies.

Made in the USA
San Bernardino, CA
17 October 2015